ONE FOR SORROW, TWO FOR JOY

A secluded house in a small Ontario town seems like the perfect safe haven for Nikki Larssen and the child she's sworn to protect — until a stranger shows up. With his career in ruins, reporter Gren Wilder returns to Vinegar Hill. He needs solitude, but what he gets is a ready-made family. Gren forms a reluctant liaison with the enigmatic woman and child who've laid claim to his home — and his heart. But Nikki is keeping secrets — and Gren has a nose for news . . .

CHERYL COOKE HARRINGTON

ONE FOR SORROW, TWO FOR JOY

Complete and Unabridged

LINFORD
Leicester

First published in the
United States of America in 1999

First Linford Edition
published 2002

All characters in this book have no existence
outside the imagination of the author, and have no
relation whatever to anyone bearing the same name
or names. These characters are not even distantly
inspired by any individual known or unknown to
the author, and all incidents are pure invention.

British Library CIP Data

Harrington, Cheryl Cooke
    One for sorrow, two for joy.—Large print ed.—
Linford romance library
    1. Love stories
    2. Large type books
    I. Title
    813.5′4 [F]

ISBN 0–7089–9879–8

Published by
F. A. Thorpe (Publishing)
Anstey, Leicestershire

Set by Words & Graphics Ltd.
Anstey, Leicestershire
Printed and bound in Great Britain by
T. J. International Ltd., Padstow, Cornwall

This book is printed on acid-free paper

For Matthew

With special thanks to:

Chef Myer (skip) Goldhar
Douglas Jack, C.A.
Sheila Seabrook and Dan Bar-Zeev
Doug Kippen
Sara Oster
Linda Johnson
and the Ladies of the Train

One for sorrow
Two for joy
Three for a girl
Four for a boy
Five for silver
Six for gold
Seven for a secret
Never to be told

Nursery Rhyme (Traditional)

1

It rolled up the valley on a new breeze. A sudden chill, heavy with the scent of green, growing, woodsy things. A freshening that shivered its way through town, fluttering curtains, rustling leaves, eddying dust and scraps of yesterday's paper along the cobbled gutters of Main Street. It meant there'd be rain before nightfall. A real thunder-boomer. A sure thing. Noble Bateman said so.

If there was one thing Nikki had come to count on in the eight months since she and Claire had arrived in Vinegar Hill, it was Noble Bateman's word. So it wasn't a bit surprising when the cloudless summer sky, blue as a robin's egg and ablaze with sunshine, grew dark and ominous just after seven. Not surprising that, by nine, the woods and fields beyond town were silent,

1

deserted, as if every living thing had taken shelter from the swiftly approaching storm. Not surprising, but damned unsettling.

Maybe it was just her imagination playing tricks on her — understandable after months of watching her back, running from every shadow. Was she wrong to let herself feel safe again? she wondered, running her mental checklist for what seemed like the millionth time. Had she left a trail? No way. No credit, no letters, not even a phone call. She'd disappeared without a word to anyone. Not that there was anyone left to care. Had she slipped up, used their real names, even once? Not a chance. Sometimes she almost forgot she'd ever had another name. Nikki and Claire Larssen were second nature to her now.

So relax. No mistakes. It was just the wild August weather that had her nerves on edge. Just the threatening rumble of thunder making those goose bumps prickle up the back of her neck.

Spooky feeling. But life in this particular house had more than its share of spooky moments, even in the bright light of day.

Nikki hesitated at the bedroom window, twisting a strand of hair around her finger, afraid to watch but equally afraid to turn away, as the storm swept out of the northwest. Not just rain, but a wind-borne river of water, as if the air itself had turned to liquid. Lightning blazed across the sky, raw power, so nerve-rackingly close that each clap of thunder set the window-panes rattling.

It was nothing short of a miracle that Claire managed to sleep through the din, she thought, forcing herself to pull the shade and draw the heavy curtains across the window. She'd been meaning to take those curtains down, replace them with something bright and airy. But, for tonight at least, she was almost glad to have the green velvet drapery with its old-fashioned tassels holding the storm at bay.

Surely Mr. Wilder wouldn't mind if she brightened up the baby's room a bit. The man couldn't possibly be as grim and humorless as the portrait that graced the parlor wall downstairs. Could he?

Another roll of thunder shook the house, made her jump, edgy as a cat in a canoe, as Noble would say. The man had a folksy saying for everything. What was it he'd said about Grenville Wilder? That his life was a sorrowful story . . . break your heart, like a sad country song. Someday he'd get around to telling her all about it. Hopefully before Mr. Wilder decided to stop his wandering and show up on her doorstep. *His* doorstep, that is.

Forget someday. She'd make a point of asking about Grenville Wilder's sorrowful story — *tomorrow*. If anyone knew the truth about old man Wilder and his gloomy house, it would be her neighbor, Noble Bateman. At seventy-three he was a walking, talking history of Vinegar Hill. Proud of it, too. There

4

wasn't a local saga, rumor or true, that Noble hadn't told, or had a hand in creating. Except, as he'd so often complained, for her own.

Too bad, she thought, tucking the well-twisted strand of hair behind her ear. Noble was a good man — solid, sensible, trustworthy — the first and only person she'd really felt she could trust since this whole, awful mess had begun. Someday, maybe, she'd be able to answer his questions, once she was sure the truth wouldn't put him in danger. In the meantime, if the worst happened, she might be very glad of a friend like Noble Bateman.

Another crash, another rattle of windows. Propping her elbows on the crib rail, Nikki rested her chin in her hands and marveled once again that Claire was still sleeping, one little thumb tucked into her mouth, one tiny finger curled over the end of her turned-up nose. Angelic . . . at least in sleep, with plump rosy cheeks, and a mop of curly black hair that shone like a raven's wing in the sunshine. *Whoa!* Where the heck had that come from? She was even beginning to think like Noble.

Thunder rolled, followed a split-second later by the sharp and unmistakable slam of the kitchen door. Just the wind? Or was someone in the house? *Impossible.* She was absolutely certain she'd locked that door.

Another bump, a sudden wash of light at the bottom of the stairs, and every doubt vanished. *They weren't alone.*

Breath caught in her throat as she turned toward the nursery door, every fibre of her being focused on the stairwell beyond, waiting for the first footfall, the first creak of old wood ... the beginning of their end. *No!* Tearing her gaze away from the doorway, she stared at Claire for a moment, then at the telephone on the dresser. Help was just minutes away, but did she dare make the call? Would things really be any different here? She crossed the room, jerked the receiver out of its cradle. What choice did she have?

White-knuckled, Nikki clutched the phone to her ear. No dial tone. Just hollow . . . empty . . . nothing. This couldn't be happening. *Not now.* Fear kept her rooted to the spot. But only for an instant, a single missed heartbeat. Then instinct kicked in. It wasn't over. Not yet. No matter what happened, she had to protect Claire, keep her safe, *survive.* She would not give up without a fight.

Crossing the room, swift and silent, Nikki paused only long enough to lock the nursery door, slipping the key into the pocket of her jeans as she tiptoed across the hallway. She paused again at the top of the stairs, trying to make sense of the growing disturbance in the kitchen. Comfortably domestic sounds, a slammed cupboard door, the clatter of pots and pans. And a faint, tempting aroma, as if . . . was somebody actually making coffee?

No way. People didn't break into a house to make coffee. But, if her instincts were right, this wasn't just *any* intruder. Make that intruders. He wouldn't come alone. No, he'd bring someone else along to do his dirty work. And make his coffee. Her mind raced. She had to get down to the kitchen, find out exactly what she was up against. Trouble was, they'd be certain to hear her coming. The creaky old staircase would announce her presence the moment she set foot on the first tread. Unless . . .

Holding her breath, she flattened herself against the wall. She'd be ready at the next flash of lightning, time her flight down the stairs to the thunder's roll, let the storm cover the sound of her approach. Then, unless one of them happened to be looking directly at the kitchen door when she got to the bottom, she'd be able to take cover, to see without being seen.

As if on cue, another bolt split the

heavens, close enough that the answering boom of thunder was immediate, and loud. Another window rattler. The kitchen lights dimmed as her foot hit the last step. Dimmed, flickered weakly, and died. She hugged the doorjamb and steadied her breath — or tried to. If she gave them what they wanted, would they leave her alone? Would they try to take Claire?

'*Well, damn,*' growled a low masculine voice, then someone in the kitchen struck a match. A faint glimmer of light drew Nikki's gaze. Broad shoulders and gleaming wet flesh held it. She watched as the stranger lit the trio of candles she kept on the counter by the sink, watched the flickering light play across his bare arms and muscular back, heard him gasp when the flame singed his fingers. He muttered another curse, then finished peeling off his shirt.

Naked to the waist and dripping wet, the man looked more like a lost lifeguard than one of Frank Medici's hired thugs. Her gaze followed the tangle of hair that straggled down his neck, lingered on a cluster of shimmering droplets caught in the small of his back, strayed lower to worn denim jeans, clinging damply to lean hips and long, powerful legs. Legs that could probably span the distance between them in two strides.

Forcing herself to look away, she scanned the room. A pair of hiking boots, muddy and worn at the heel, lay just inside the door, with sodden socks and a sorry-looking hat tossed in a heap beside them. The only other item of note, an enormous canvas duffel bag, had been dumped in the middle of the floor, blocking passage to the dining room. Despite all the clatter a moment ago, she could find no hint that the broad-shouldered stranger had brought any backup. Small favor. The man was formidable enough on his own. And, with only one way down from the second floor, there was absolutely no way she'd ever sneak past him with Claire.

He reached for a towel and Nikki made her move. Arming herself with the largest, heaviest, meanest-looking cast-iron frying pan from the rack on the wall, she crept silently across the room.

He threw the towel over his head as she drew near, using both hands to wring the rainwater out of his hair. He seemed even bigger with his arms raised. Was she completely crazy? What if she missed? How hard did you have to hit someone to knock them out? And what if she hit him too hard? Would she kill him? *Definitely crazy*. But it was too late to turn back now. She drew a deep, silent breath. Aware of the faint musky scent of him, the slow ripple of his muscles in the candlelight, she tightened her grip on the skillet.

The man breathed a low sigh, rolling his shoulders and neck in a long, easy stretch as he dropped the wet towel into the sink. He yawned, fumbled with his belt buckle, obviously about to shed the rest of his wet clothes.

It was now or never, she told herself, imagining his fingers on the zipper, his jeans sliding slowly to the floor. *Stop him!* Her heart clattered against her ribs, blood roared in her ears, loud enough to drown out the sound of the storm that still raged outside. Do it. *Do it now!*

She swung, grimacing with effort, wielding the skillet like a baseball bat as the stranger turned toward her. Nikki saw him register an instant of surprise, or maybe fright, before the heavy pan connected with his skull. It made a sound like an overripe melon dropped on the sidewalk. She sucked back a scream.

He didn't fall right away. Just tottered unsteadily for a long, breathless moment. And he didn't look dead. Far from it. He looked . . . he looked really pissed-off.

The man took a single step toward her, groaned, then crumpled like Claire's favorite rag doll and sank slowly onto the floor.

Now what? *Move!* Too late. His well-placed kick swept her feet right out from under her. She hit the floor with a thud that jarred her teeth and drove the breath from her lungs.

'Ow, uh-uhhh.' The stranger groaned again as he rolled awkwardly toward her. Wrenching the frying pan out of her hands, he sent it skittering across the wet floor. Cold fingers tightened around her wrist as he leaned close. 'Who are you?' he demanded. 'And what the *hell* are you doing in my house?'

'*Your house?*' Twisting free, Nikki scrambled to her feet. 'What do you mean, *your* house?'

He was holding his head in his hands now, still groaning, but she'd seen enough to be certain he was *not* Grenville Wilder. Not unless he'd found the fountain of youth, or had some kind of Dorian Gray thing going with that old portrait in the parlor.

Another clap of thunder shook the house, quickly followed by a loud moan from the man on the floor, and a shrill cry from the room above.

Oh, please, not now, thought Nikki, willing the child to be quiet for just a while longer. No use. Claire's frightened cry erupted into a full-fledged wail as the lightning flashed again.

The stranger stopped groaning and listened. Watching his expression, she had the fleeting impression of pain — not the kind of pain inflicted by a cast iron pan, but a deeper, more personal sort of pain. He looked up at her as he struggled to his feet, and the moment of vulnerability vanished.

Nikki kept her distance, backing slowly toward the stairs. The man staggered across the room, stopping to rest with one hand on the fridge door. He sure knew how to act as if he owned the place. Was it possible? A glimmer of hope sparked to life. Maybe her worst nightmare hadn't come true, after all. Maybe the cover she'd so carefully created to protect little Claire was still intact. But if the half-naked man in her kitchen wasn't a Medici thug, who was he? And what did he want?

'You nearly took my head off,' he grumbled, pulling a tray of ice from the freezer, wincing with the effort of turning to face her again. Upstairs, Claire howled.

'Well?' he snapped, 'What are you waiting for?'

'What? I — ' Nikki glared at him as the heart-stopping fear of a moment ago gave way to anger. A much more useful emotion. What did he expect her to do? Beg for their lives, maybe? Or clear out in the middle of the worst rainstorm of the century with a nine-month-old baby in tow? He'd wait a long time on either count.

'Well?' he repeated, moving slowly back to the sink. 'Are you going to take care of that squalling brat, or do I have to do it myself?'

'You stay away from her! And from me!' *Cool it!* Why was she letting him push all her buttons? Even if it really was his house, the man had no business barging in the way he had, unannounced, in the middle of the night. She wasn't the one in the wrong, here. Grabbing another skillet from the rack, she waved it in his direction. 'I want you out of here. *Right now!*'

The stranger stared at her for a long moment, seemingly mystified. Then, muttering under his breath and obviously in pain, he slowly turned his back. Nikki watched as he pulled a plastic bag out of the drawer beside the sink and dumped the tray of ice cubes into it. Giving the top a twist, he held it ever-so-gingerly to the side of his head.

'Hear this,' he said at last, turning slowly back to face her. 'Somebody's going to be leaving this house tonight. But, Lady, it *won't* be me.'

★   ★   ★

'It's okay, pumpkin, it's okay. See? I brought us a twinkle light.' The flame shivered as she placed the tiny, glass-sheathed candle on the dresser,

16

sending ripples of light and shadow dancing across Claire's tear-streaked face. Arms outstretched, the baby gave another shuddering sob.

'It's just a noisy old storm. Nothing to be afraid of.' Nothing but a raving lunatic in the kitchen, that is. Nikki scooped the whimpering child into her arms. She wasn't about to leave the man alone down there, but she couldn't leave Claire alone, either. The two of them would just have to face the intruder together.

'Ga-ga, *Ga-ga,*' demanded Claire, between sobs.

'Uh-oh. Did you lose him again?' Dutifully retrieving Raggedy Man from the floor beneath the crib, she tucked him under the baby's arm. For the last few months, the old rag doll had been Claire's version of a security blanket, and she latched onto it now, clutching its yellow, woolly hair with one fist and the collar of Nikki's white T-shirt with the other. 'Ga-ga,' she said again, forgetting to cry this time.

Lightning flashed, thunder rolled. A bit farther away now, but the rain still hammered against the windowpanes, the wind still howled around the eaves. Content to be held, Claire seemed oblivious.

Fleetingly, Nikki let herself consider how wonderful it must be to have someone you knew you could count on, someone to make everything all right, to keep you safe. And then she sighed resignedly. In all her twenty-four years, at least all that she could remember, there hadn't been a single soul who'd fit that bill. Not one person who hadn't let her down. No one to count on but herself.

She drew a deep breath and squared her shoulders, offering up a silent prayer that Claire would never regret counting on her, that her instincts about the man in the kitchen were right. Would a thug bother to kick off his muddy boots at the door? Would a man with murder on his mind take time to dry off and make coffee?

Who are you, and what the hell are you doing in my house? If he was lying, the man was one heck of a good actor.

'Guess we'd better get you a dry diaper, eh, pumpkin? And then we're going downstairs. You, me, and Raggedy Man. We've got some company to take care of.'

His house. If it was, she'd have some explaining to do. If not, she'd be ready to run, ready to fight, ready to do whatever it took to keep Claire safe.

The baby yawned. In another minute or two, she'd probably remember she was hungry and demand her midnight bottle. How the heck did you warm up a bottle during a power failure? No stove, no microwave . . . no water. The pump would be off line, too. Nikki sighed again as she fastened the diaper. It was one crisis after another in the 'mommy' business, and things were definitely learn-as-you-go. Kids should come with operating instructions. And a warning . . . *assembly required*.

Leaving the candle twinkling on

Claire's dresser, she felt her way across the dark hallway and down the stairs, cradling the baby in one arm. It seemed their uninvited guest was managing quite well on his own, she decided, as they neared the kitchen door. Apparently he'd found the stash of emergency candles she kept under the sink, because the room was now aglow with warm light, alive with playful shadows. She noticed his big duffel bag next. It seemed to have exploded, spewing socks, shirts, and who-knew-what-else in a jumble across the floor. His wet jeans had been added to the pile of sodden clothing at the door.

Oh, please, don't let him be standing there in his undershorts, she thought, striding bravely into the room — at least, as bravely as her hammering heart would allow. She found him lounging comfortably on a chair at the end of the kitchen table, wearing another pair of tattered jeans, topped with a wrinkled, half-buttoned, red plaid shirt. His tousled hair had dried in a honey-colored tangle that disappeared under his collar. Legs crossed at the ankle, he rested his slender, bare feet on the rungs of Claire's highchair.

'Making himself right at home, isn't he, pumpkin?' she whispered, watching as he poured a generous serving of Mr. Wilder's twenty-five-year-old Scotch whisky into a crystal tumbler, a combination that sparkled like gold and diamonds in the flickering candlelight. Before she could comment on his terrible manners, he popped one of her specialty crab rolls into his mouth and smiled contentedly.

'Mmmm,' he said, reaching for another. 'That hit the spot.'

'*What are you doing? You can't eat those!*' Balancing the suddenly wide awake and wide-eyed Claire on her hip, Nikki raced across the room to snatch the plate of food off the table. She'd worked all afternoon on those crab rolls, intended for tomorrow's garden party at Ravensleigh, not a quickie midnight snack. And if the food order was short, even by two tiny crab rolls, Mrs. Beckett would be sure to complain.

'Tasted perfectly edible to me,' he said, taking a long, easy swallow of whisky.

'You might have asked first! What do you think you're doing, scarfing down my hors-d'oeuvres and guzzling Mr. Wilder's good Scotch? Who do you think you are, anyway? And you'd better tell me the truth this time, or . . . or I'm calling the police.'

'Be my guest,' said the stranger, with a magnanimous wave toward the telephone. 'But I wouldn't get your hopes up.'

'What?'

'Phone's dead.'

He knew. 'D-dead?' *Damn!* Why had she let that tremor creep into her voice. She made herself stand a little straighter. If he could act tough, so could she. 'Storm must've knocked it out.'

'I suppose. In any case, there'll be no police running to the rescue of either one of us tonight, I'm afraid.'

Without another word, the man unfolded his legs, pushed to his feet, and strode away from her, carrying his glass and Mr. Wilder's bottle of Scotch.

'Where do you think you're going?'

He turned, raising one eyebrow, as if surprised to be asked. 'I'm going to get some sleep, Miss . . . whoever-you-are. Perhaps you should do the same.'

'You are *not* going to sleep in my house!'

'Your house?' Both eyebrows arched this time.

'Well, I . . . I'm responsible for it. The owner's counting on me to — '

The stranger cut her off with a low, rumbling laugh, as darkly disturbing as the thunder still rolling overhead. 'I'm counting on you, am I? Don't know about that. What I *am* doing, I'd say, is taking a chance on you. You can stay . . . just for tonight . . . but don't thank me. Thank the storm. *Nobody* deserves to be put out in that.'

All right. Enough was enough. This guy needed some serious straightening out. Nikki settled Claire and her Raggedy Man into the highchair and turned to confront him again.

'I've had enough of your attitude, Mister. Tell me who you are, *right now*. And don't think you can fool me. The owner of this house is a famous author.'

'Famous? Well, thank you very much, I'm sure. That's probably the nicest thing anyone's said to me this year.' Wearing a wry little smile, he crossed the room again. 'Gren Wilder, at your service. And you are?'

Nikki found herself backing away as he moved toward her, backing away until her hips touched the edge of the counter and she could go no farther. He didn't stop, advancing until he stood mere inches from her suddenly trembling body. So close . . .

She stared at his chest, at a row of tortoiseshell buttons on a sea of plaid, watched them rise and fall with each breath he took, remembered him shirtless, dripping rainwater, gleaming in the candlelight. Too close! She could feel his heat through the red flannel.

Forcing herself to look up at his weary, stubbled face, she studied the eyes that stared inscrutably back at her. It was impossible to guess their color. By candlelight they seemed black and utterly bottomless, circled by deep, darkening hollows. It must have been a very long time since he'd slept, she thought, unable to look away. She could smell the Scotch on his breath, apple-sweet and sharp. Maybe that explained the haggard expression. Maybe whisky was a habit.

Nikki's breath caught in her throat as he leaned toward her, his tongue sliding across his lips in a slow, seductive gesture. He pressed closer. *Move!*

Ducking under his arm, she skipped out of reach, watching as he set the crystal glass on the counter beside the sink. Was that all he'd intended to do? Just get rid of a dirty glass? Nothing threatening about that, was there? So why on earth was she still trembling?

Planting herself firmly between Claire and the scruffy stranger who claimed to be Gren Wilder, she tried her best to look brave, or at least composed. She felt anything but. Her heart stammered and her mouth felt cottony-dry. And to make matters worse, the man was smiling again, as if seeing her so thoroughly uncomfortable was the highlight of his day.

'You are *not* Grenville Wilder,' she said, trying to recall every detail of the portrait in the parlor. 'Grenville Wilder is an old man. He writes boring, stuffy books about . . . about economic theory and . . . and . . . '

The stranger laughed. 'My father was a well-respected authority on economics. And those boring, stuffy books of his are still required reading in some of the best schools.'

Offering his hand, he grinned, almost mischievously. 'Gren Wilder, son of the famous Doctor Grenville Wilder. Also a writer . . . not quite so famous . . . somewhat less boring. I hope, anyway.'

Nikki felt her jaw drop and, when it did, Gren Wilder laughed again. 'I haven't spent much time here lately, but this is my place now. My father passed away nearly ten years ago.' Sinking back onto his chair, Gren picked up the makeshift icebag and held it to his head.

'Ga-ga!' Claire leaned forward in her highchair, pointing at him and bouncing happily. 'Ga-ga, Ga-ga, *Ga-ga*,' she repeated, at the top of her lungs.

Nikki frowned. Gren Wilder did, indeed, look a lot like Raggedy Man, she decided, comparing his straggly honey-brown hair, red shirt, and threadbare jeans to Claire's beloved ragamuffin doll. And, in that instant of forgotten anger before his smile faded away, she could almost imagine him loveable. *Almost.*

Gren studied the baby for a long moment, a puzzled, wistful expression on his face, then took another swig of Scotch, straight from the bottle this time.

'The way I see it,' he grumbled, 'you're either a trespasser, and a damned good liar, or you're the new Mrs. Hoskett. So? Which is it? And be careful what you say. I expect proof.'

2

What did the child see? he wondered, touching his lips to the whisky bottle again. What was so interesting that she couldn't look away?

The baby smiled, gurgling at him through the tiny fist balled up in her mouth. He was tempted, briefly, to smile back, but scowled instead. What had Aprile been thinking, bringing a child into this house? It wasn't right.

Gren longed to tip the bottle, to let the amber liquid trickle into his mouth and down his throat, smooth comfort, like satin sheets. But those wide, innocent baby eyes held him in thrall. Where had she come from, this tiny sprout of a person who ogled him in open-mouthed wonder, making him remember who he was and why he'd come home? It was almost as if she knew.

Setting the bottle on the table unsipped, he drew the back of his hand across his mouth. Whiskers, two day's worth, rasped against his skin. No wonder the sprout was so fascinated, he thought, imagining what he must look like to her — a wild apparition, like nothing she'd ever seen before. The smile she'd been trying to coax out of him flickered briefly across his face. Suddenly, her mother's frying-pan-to-the-head reaction to his surprise arrival wasn't so hard to understand.

He shifted his gaze across the room. Unfazed by the power failure, mother had coaxed enough hot water from the tap to warm up a bottle of milk for the child. Now she waited, tapping her foot, pretending she hadn't been watching him, pretending she wasn't scared half to death. Quite a woman. Make that girl. He sensed a certain naivete about her that, coupled with her slim, boyish figure and elfin features, made her seem barely old enough to take care of herself, let alone a child. Strange, though. Maybe he'd been chasing stories for too many years, or maybe it was just the shock of finding these particular strangers in his home, but whatever the reason, he couldn't help thinking he was seeing exactly what she wanted him to see.

He studied her, unnoticed, as she played with her hair, twisting a lock around her finger, unwinding it slowly, then twisting again. Black as midnight, just like the sprout's hair, but straight. And she'd cropped it short so it barely skimmed the delicate line of her jaw, a gamin style she might have cut herself. In the flickering candlelight, her face looked porcelain-pale, her lips blood red. His fault? Had he frightened her that badly?

She dribbled a bit of milk onto the inside of her wrist, then lifted it to her mouth, parting her lips, drawing the warm liquid onto her tongue . . . an incredibly sensual gesture and so achingly familiar, it stole his breath away.

She caught him watching when she looked up and tried to ignore him, drying her wrist on the front of her white T-shirt, tucking her hair behind her ear with an impatient motion as she crossed the room.

'Here you go, pumpkin,' she crooned, bending to drop a kiss on the baby's cheek. 'Just the way you like it. We'll put Raggedy Man beside you, okay?' She lingered for a moment, touching the child's cheek, brushing a wisp of hair from her face, before turning slowly back to face him.

'Are you really Grenville Wilder?' she asked, sinking onto the chair opposite his, propping her elbows on the table. She rested her chin in her hands and narrowed her eyes, looking doubtful, anxious, and *very* young.

'In the flesh,' answered Gren, slapping his driver's licence onto the table in front of her. 'Not the greatest picture, but I think it proves my point.'

She poked at the plastic card with one finger, then pulled away, folding her hands in her lap, sitting a little straighter. She was obviously nervous, and rightfully so. After all, only minutes ago she'd attempted to murder her boss. Of course, at the time, she hadn't known . . .

'Well?' he asked, letting her squirm, enjoying a moment's revenge for the blazing headache she'd given him. 'I'd say you've had long enough to think things over. What's it gonna be? Are you a liar . . . or the new Mrs. Hoskett?'

The overhead lights sparked to life as he spoke, chasing shadows, flooding the room with eye-smarting brilliance.

'Given the choices, I guess I'm the new Mrs. Hoskett,' she answered, twisting another strand of hair as she squinted across the table at him. 'My name's Nikki, and this is Claire.' She glanced at the child who gurgled happily, thumping her half-empty bottle against the highchair. 'Mrs. Massey said — '

'My sister,' he interrupted, just to be certain she had no lingering doubts about his identity.

'Pardon me?'

'Aprile Massey is my sister.'

'Yes. That's what she said.' As her eyes adjusted to the light, Nikki scrutinized him with an intensity that left him feeling like a bug on a pin. What was she looking for?

'She also told me the former housekeeper was getting on in years. This big house was too much for her, I guess. She decided to retire.'

'Ga-ga, *Ga-ga*!' screeched Claire, dropping the rag doll over the side of the highchair, then torpedoing it with her bottle. Nikki retrieved both, wiped the baby's chin, and tucked Raggedy Man under her arm once again. All the while, her gaze remained locked on Gren's face.

'Hoskett retired?' Breaking eye contact, he glanced briefly at the whisky bottle, curling his fingers around the neck, pulling it close. What had he expected? That things would be just as he'd left them, old Mrs. Hoskett included? It had been five years, nearly six. Things changed. *He'd* changed . . . become a stranger in his own home.

Tipping the bottle, he took a long, slow swallow, and found Nikki glaring at him when he looked back. Disapproving. Judging. Who the hell did she think she was? He pulled a packet of Players from his shirt pocket, tapped it on the table, peeled off the cellophane wrapper.

'So, Aprile hired you, did she?' Lifting the pack to his lips he extracted a cigarette, offering a muttered opinion of Aprile's decision. '*Huh.*'

'What's that supposed to mean?'

'It means you don't look halfway big enough to do a proper job,' he said, fingering the cigarette, trying to imagine her scrubbing floors or washing windows. She didn't look the type. No, something about this just didn't feel right. But what? He dredged in his pocket for a match.

'I'm quite capable of taking care of myself *and* this house.' *And you,* her tone seemed to imply. She reached across the table to snatch the cigarette from his hand.

'*What the* — '

'If you want to smoke, you'll have to take it outside. It wouldn't be good for Claire.'

He winced. There was no arguing with that. But the baby had been so quiet for the past few minutes, half asleep, with her head on that old rag doll, he'd almost forgotten she was in the room. Barely resisting the urge to take another drink, he lifted the ice bag to his temple instead.

'All right, uh . . . Nikki, is it?'

She nodded, a glimmer of surprise lighting her clear, green eyes. Apparently she hadn't expected to win the cigarette war so easily. She had no idea she'd done them both a favor. No way of knowing he'd finally quit the habit two weeks ago, or that it was still a struggle for him to get through the day without a smoke. A second's delay on her part and he could have blamed the lapse on her. 'How long have you been here? D'you have a last name? Some ID, maybe?'

'Larssen,' she said, in a voice almost as cold as her suddenly icy stare.

He gave in, taking another slug from the bottle. Nikki Larssen? No . . . something wrong there. The name didn't fit. Ten years of reporting for the top newspapers in the country had taught him a thing or two about listening to people. Not just what they said, but how they said it. The silence between the words. And he knew a lie when he heard one. What was she up to, this dark-haired wisp of a girl?

'My ID's upstairs . . . somewhere. Guess you'll just have to trust me.'

'Trust you? Lady, you just tried to kill me in my own house! Why the *hell* should I trust you?'

Watching the color bloom on her cheeks, Gren felt a moment of shame for treating her so badly. It was a very brief moment, though. She straightened abruptly, gripping the edge of the table, her cool gaze colliding with his.

'And what would you have done? You could've been a maniac, for all I knew. Your sister didn't expect you back. Said you were traveling, seeing the world. Research or something. For a book.'

'Charitable of her,' mumbled Gren, recalling the truth of his fall into the bottle. 'Not quite so pleasant as she made it seem, I'm afraid. But, yes. I plan to write again. Came home for some peace and quiet.' He glanced at Claire. 'Think you and the kid can stay out of my way?'

He watched her hands clench again but, to her credit, she kept her voice steady, almost managed a smile to go along with her reply.

'We'll try to blend into the wood-work, Mr. Wilder.'

Not much chance of that, he thought, swallowing a laugh, surprised to find himself imagining how a real smile would light up her face. 'Fine. We'll give it a week. I take breakfast at eight, nothing fancy. Dinner at seven.

Here in the kitchen will be fine. Oh, and there's a month's worth of dirty laundry in the duffel bag. I'd suggest you get at it before it molders. Most of it's soaked through.'

If the prospect bothered her, Nikki hid it well. Smiling, she turned to lift the baby out of her highchair, whispering something he couldn't quite understand.

'Will that be all . . . *sir?*'

'It's Gren. I'll, um . . . I'll let you know if I need anything else. Good night, Nikki. And Claire.'

'Good night, *Mister* Wilder.'

Beautiful, tough, and *very* angry. Was it all men? he wondered. Or just the ones who tried to scare her to death in the middle of the night?

Suddenly her anger didn't matter. He didn't want her to go, didn't want her to walk up those stairs. If she left him alone, he'd have to face the silence . . . four walls, and a lifetime of memories . . . ghosts in the dark.

'Nikki? Before you go . . . isn't there something you've forgotten to tell me?'

She stopped, stiff-shouldered, turning slowly back to face him. For just an instant, he thought he saw fear in her eyes.

'Nothing I can think of.' Her voice sounded clear and strong, unwavering, but he could feel her tension. And that icy stare again . . . it made him want to shiver.

'Those crab rolls of yours — they were *very* good, by the way. But is there something I should know? I mean, are we having a party?'

Whoa! A little crack in the armor, maybe? That compliment had almost earned him a smile. Almost, but not quite.

'No, *we* are not having a party,' she said, as if the very thought were ludicrous.

Ah, well, so much for cracks in the armor.

'I'm catering a party at Ravensleigh tomorrow, Mr. Wilder, and I'd really appreciate it if you wouldn't eat up any more of my profits. If the order is short — '

'You're a caterer? I thought you worked for me, Miss Larssen.'

Shifting little Claire to her other hip, Nikki hugged the child a bit closer, stroked her hair, and kissed her cheek, studying him all the while, as if considering her answer. 'Now that you're back, I suppose I do work for you. But up until tonight I've been working for Mrs. Massey. And she approved.'

'I see. And exactly what was it my sister approved of?'

'My business . . . *Minute Meals*.'

'*Minute Meals*? And what, pray tell, are *Minute Meals*?'

Shifting the baby again, she gave a soft and weary-sounding sigh. 'There are a lot of busy people in Vinegar Hill, Mr. Wilder. People who commute to work in Toronto every day. They don't have time to cook proper meals, so I do it for them, stock their freezers with meals for the week. Good food, ready to heat and eat. *Minute Meals*.'

'I see. And how's business?'

'Don't worry, I won't let it interfere with my work here. Tomorrow's a special case . . . a favor for one of my customers.' Drawing a deep breath, she hiked Claire up to her shoulder and continued. 'Sorry I snapped at you before . . . about the hors d'oeuvres, I mean. I guess, if you're still hungry, I could make you something . . . '

Was he imagining it, or did her voice seem a few degrees warmer? Suddenly, though, Nikki Larssen looked about as bone-weary as he felt. The sprout's tiny head was beginning to nod, too.

'More tired than hungry, right now,' he lied, hoping she wouldn't hear his stomach grumbling from across the room. 'But thanks.'

She looked relieved, let her shoulders droop a bit as she turned away. 'Good night, then.'

The sprout watched him over Nikki's shoulder as they left the room, her wide, brown eyes unblinking. A baby in Wilder House? Gren slowly shook his head. Coming home again had been hard enough, but finding them here . . .

'Good night,' he said, breathing a sigh that shivered through his body like a cold November wind. Time for bed. Another drink or two under the covers would warm him up, maybe even hold the memories at bay. It wouldn't be easy, though. Not with them in the house. Aprile had no right.

He pushed to his feet, twisting the cork back into the bottle for the trip down the hall. Maybe things weren't so different after all.

★　★　★

'*Breakfast at eight . . . nothing fancy.*' Nikki paced the length of the hallway for what had to be the hundredth time, sweeping the hair from her face with a shake of her head as she quietly mocked Gren Wilder's arrogant voice. 'Dinner at seven . . . bags of moldy laundry . . . who does he think he is?'

The all-too-obvious answer to that question stopped her in her tracks, put an end to her muttering. He was the boss. And she'd signed on as housekeeper. To an empty house, true, but she'd known he'd be coming back. Someday.

He certainly wasn't what she'd expected, though. Far from it. When Aprile Massey had talked about her brother, she'd assumed he'd be older, assumed the scowling portrait of Grenville Wilder on the parlor wall was a portrait of her boss. And she'd prepared herself to cope with a gruff and stuffy old man, not a broodingly handsome young writer. Not that he was all that young. Thirty-five, if his driver's license didn't lie. Nearly eleven years older than she. But still, not the old man she'd expected.

If his licence didn't lie . . . come to think of it, why was she so willing to believe him? Sure, he had official-looking ID to back up his claim, but then, so did she. And if a never-stepped-outside-the-law apprentice chef from Gastown could come up with a new identity in less than twenty-four hours, what was to stop Frank Medici from putting one of his own men in Gren Wilder's shoes?

Slipping quietly into the nursery, Nikki flopped onto her narrow cot and stared into the darkness, pondering her next move. The rain seemed to be letting up a bit, at last. Maybe, if she hurried, they could be packed and out of the house before eight . . . before the man came looking for his breakfast. But where would they go?

She should've had a plan ready, a way out, an escape. But instead she'd let herself believe they'd be safe here at Wilder House. It was almost as if the place had cast a spell on her. She remembered the sense of homecoming she'd felt the first time she'd stepped through the door . . . the lingering smell of gingerbread in the kitchen, the gleaming copper kettle on the stove. Eight long months ago, on a snowy January afternoon, she'd taken one look at the place and fallen in love.

Oh, the house was old and creaky, true enough. A bit dog-eared and worn at the edges, like a well-used book. Maybe that was what made it so homey, so comforting. That, and the fact that there were no nosy neighbors to worry about. A good mile past the edge of town, Wilder House stood back from the road, surrounded by cornfields and hardwood forest. Red brick, with a timeworn cedar roof and a wide wraparound porch.

Inside was a comfortable clutter, a combination of antiques and just plain 'old', unchanged since the house was built back in the thirties. Only the kitchen had been modernized, with gleaming stainless steel, warm terra cotta tiles, and a polished pine table. A cook's kitchen, but made for a family, she'd always thought. And, until tonight, she and Claire had been that family.

Nikki rolled off the bed, padded softly across the room to smile down at the sleeping child. To heck with Gren

Wilder, anyway. *If* that was really who he was. This wasn't just his home, it was theirs, too. The only home Claire had ever known.

She paced across the hall again, stopping at the top of the stairs. The house was dark and almost quiet. Just the soft patter of rain on the roof, the gentle hum of the refrigerator, and, from somewhere beyond the kitchen, in Mr. Wilder's private wing, a low, rumbling snore. He was sleeping.

Nervously catching her bottom lip between her teeth, Nikki crept down the stairs to the kitchen. Every creak of the old staircase seemed to echo through the house as if calling the man to wake up, but the slow, steady rhythm of his snore remained unbroken.

She took a chance, hit the light switch, stared at the closed door at the far end of the kitchen. *'My brother's private rooms,'* Mrs. Massey had said. *'He has the only key. Please respect his privacy.'* And Nikki had done just that. In fact, until this very moment, she hadn't been the least bit curious to know what lay beyond. One stroke in his favor. He did have the key . . . or he'd picked the lock. She sighed. Were all these doubts reasonable suspicion or mad paranoia?

Her gaze fell on his duffel bag next, and the clothing still strewn across the floor in a tangle. She crossed the room, fell on her knees beside the bag, and tugged on the half-open zipper . . . stuck fast.

A month's worth of dirty laundry, eh? Nikki wrinkled her nose. It did have a rather distinctive odor, somewhere between wet dogs and ripe gym lockers. She sighed. This was no time to be squeamish. And anyway, how bad could it be?

Slipping her hand inside, she rummaged past wads of damp clothing, past cold, plastic-wrapped packets that felt like books and audiotapes, until her fingers closed around something smooth and dry. Pulling a black vinyl pouch from the depths, she sprang to her feet, quickly putting some space between herself and Gren Wilder's moldy laundry.

The pouch held half a dozen spiral notebooks, filled cover-to-cover with an impossible-to-read scrawl, as cryptic as the man who'd penned it. With them was a boarding pass for 'Wilder, G.' clipped to a ticket stub for an Air France flight from Paris to Toronto, dated yesterday. And his passport. She flipped through the pages. He'd been seeing the world all right, collecting visa stamps from countries in Africa, the middle east, and Europe. Not your typical tourist destinations, either, but places like Palestine and Bosnia.

Gren Wilder, clean-shaven, hair shorn and neatly combed, stared back at her from page two, looking enough like the gruff old man in the portrait to be his son, she supposed. Same strong jaw, same determined set to the mouth. His eyes were different though, not glinting and hawkish like the old man. She felt drawn to his eyes, just as she had been hours before, here in the kitchen. Deep, bottomless pools . . . and so sad, so haunted. What was his 'sorrowful story'?

Of course! Noble Bateman would know the truth. By morning the phones would be back on line and she'd have her answers. Maybe, if the stranger really was who he claimed to be, she'd give him his week . . . for Claire's sake. They had nothing to lose. And how much trouble could one man be, after all?

3

'Calm . . . will you . . . calm . . . Aprile?
Aw, for . . . ' Gren moaned softly into
the pillow as he dragged the phone
away from his ear. Sweeping his fingers
across the throbbing goose-egg on his
temple, he closed his eyes against the
glare of early morning sun and the
drone of Aprile's voice. Once — just
once — he wished his sister would stop
her nattering and listen. But the woman
blathered on, question after question
with no pause for reply. Not that there
was any need to reply. Given a moment
or two, Aprile would voice her own
answers and inform him later that he'd
said so-and-so about this-or-that, and
why on earth didn't he remember?

He groaned again, audibly this time.
Except for the headache, this conversation was identical to the last one he'd
had with his big sister. And the one

before that, too. Wondering how long it would take her to realize he'd stopped listening. Gren wrestled the top off an aspirin bottle and swallowed two tablets, dry. Another day, he might have considered washing them down with a swig from the bottle on the bedside table, but this wasn't a hair-of-the-dog situation. No, this particular headache — the mother of all headaches — had nothing whatsoever to do with the pint of scotch he'd consumed last night. This one was definitely impact-induced, courtesy of Nikki Larssen and her frying pan.

Had she intended to kill him? Huh. He might have been better off if she had. The lump on his temple pulsed with every heartbeat, hot and painfully tender. It was going to take more than a couple of aspirin to make him feel better. A lot more.

Answers were what he needed. Answers only Aprile knew. All the whys and wherefores of Nikki Larssen, the wild-eyed super-mom who'd laid claim to his house. And he needed those answers now . . . before he took his life in his hands again and ventured out into her kitchen. *His* kitchen, he reminded himself. If only his sister would . . . ahhh, silence. Easing the phone back up to his ear, he heard Aprile sigh. Loudly.

'All right, little brother,' she said at last, 'I get the point. It's just . . . well, I'm happy to hear your voice, that's all. It's been so long. And . . . Gren? Grenville? Are you there?'

To his surprise, Gren found himself smiling into the phone. He was home all right, and beginning to enjoy himself, despite the killer headache. He'd been playing this particular game with his sister for as long as he could remember. She'd get on his case, he'd tune her out. Always did drive her crazy. He could almost see her now . . . forehead furrowed, those perfectly pencilled eyebrows of hers knitting together . . .

'*Gren!*'

'Speak softly, dear sister. I have a headache.'

'A headache? Oh, Gren, you . . . you haven't been —

'Don't go there, Aprile.' A lecture was not part of his plan for the morning. Especially not *that* lecture. He wasn't a drunk. Not anymore. He'd put an end to that part of his life weeks ago and half a world away. Until last night that is. Until Nikki and Claire, and all the memories.

'What? Don't go where? Gren? What on earth are you talking about?'

'The Aprile Wilder lecture series. I'm not in the mood. Might have to put the phone down again.'

'You *know* how I hate that,' she muttered, so obviously indignant, he couldn't help but smile.

'Self defense, sis.'

'Uh-huh. Well? I'm listening. What's so important you can't take a minute to talk to your only sister?'

'Nikki Larssen.'

'Nikki?' Aprile's voice brightened

noticeably. 'Such a dear. We're lucky to have her, you know. How is she?'

'She's doing just fine, from what I can tell . . . hell of a lot better than me.'

'What? What d'you mean?'

'The woman tried to kill me last night.'

'*What?*'

Too late, Gren jerked the phone away from his ear. His sister's shriek of disbelief sent pain spiking through the top of his head.

'You heard me.' He swallowed the curse that threatened to erupt. Swallowed the urge to give Aprile a piece of his mind, too. After all, her intentions had been good . . . though, as usual, not particularly well thought out. *Proceed with caution.* 'Where did you find her, Aprile? And exactly what do you know about her?'

'She . . . Gren, what do you mean she tried to kill you? How?'

'Walloped me with a frying pan. And that, dear sister, is the reason for this blasted headache. The woman's a lunatic, if you ask me.'

'She . . . hit you? But why . . . Gren, I don't understand. Why would Nikki hit you?'

'Said she thought I was breaking in, then ordered me out of my own home. She'd have whacked me again if I hadn't managed to get the freakin' pan out of her hand. Dammit, Aprile, I came home expecting to find some peace, a quiet house, a place to write, to concentrate . . . just me and good old Mrs. Hoskett . . . '

'Oh, dear . . . it's the baby, isn't it? I'm so sorry, Gren. But you needn't swear at me. We didn't expect you back. I assumed you'd contact me first, that I'd be able to explain, to prepare you . . . '

'Explain *now*, Aprile.'

He sounded too gruff, too impatient, the words a mirror image of his mood. But what did she expect? Did she honestly believe she could have pre-pared him for this? It wasn't just the baby, or the crazy mother, either. It was

. . . *everything.* Too much had changed. '*Well?*'

'Please, Gren, calm down. It hasn't been easy for me, either, you know. And when Mrs. Hoskett retired . . . well, I thought I'd never find anybody willing to take on the job. The old place is so lonely.'

'*Exactly.* Why on earth would a young woman like Nikki Larssen want to live way out here in the middle of nowhere? What's her story, anyway?'

'Well . . . she's highly qualified.'

'To do what?'

'Before the baby came she was an apprentice chef. I met her last winter, just after she got to Toronto. She was working a party for my caterer, trying to hide the fact that she'd brought little Claire along with her . . . what a sweet child.'

Gren chuckled to himself. Seemed he wasn't the only Wilder who'd been charmed by the sprout. 'So, what did you do, Sis? Hire her on the spot?'

'Well . . . '

'Oh, boy. You did, didn't you? No references? No background check?'

'*Character*, little brother. I pride myself on being a fine judge of it. And your Nikki hasn't disappointed me.'

My Nikki?

'The house is spotless, everything neat as a pin. Well . . . isn't it?' As usual, Aprile didn't wait for an answer. 'And her cooking! Mmmmmmm.' She paused, as if giving her next words some careful consideration. 'Why don't I join the two of you for dinner tonight?'

Dinner? *Bad idea*. This phone call was bad enough. He was far from ready to cope with Aprile's meddling face-to-face. 'Hmmm. Maybe next week. If *your* Nikki lasts that long.'

'If — What's that supposed to mean?'

'I gave her a week — don't start with me, Aprile.' She'd had her chance. This time his sister would listen to him. 'She's lucky I didn't throw her out last night, what with the murder attempt and all. Might've, too, except for the storm.' And the sprout, he thought, pausing for effect. Aprile was apparently speechless, and that was a first. Might as well go for the knockout.

'Don't really need a housekeeper anyway, now that I'm back.' There. Let her chew on that for a while.

'Don't need a housekeeper? Ha! I can see it all now . . . ace reporter, chin deep in research, dishes piling up in the sink . . . assuming you'd even remember to eat, that is.'

'Very funny.'

'You know I'm right.'

Gren felt his smile fade. Aprile's little scenario did ring uncomfortably true. Her voice was as smug as the self-satisfied smirk she was undoubtedly wearing. A change of subject was *way* overdue.

'Y'know, I do believe I smell coffee. Must be time to say good morning to Miss Nikki.' Chuckling, he added, 'Wonder if that old football helmet of mine is still in the hall closet?'

'Football hel — Honestly, Gren! Do

try to be nice to Nikki. She's perfect for you . . . er . . . for the house. And you've no idea how hard it would be to replace her.'

'I'm sure. Like I said, I'll give her a week. Then . . . we'll see. Bye, Sis.'

Perfect for you. So that was Aprile's game. Not bloody likely. Gren dropped the phone into its cradle, retrieving his jeans and wrinkled plaid shirt from the foot of the bed. He was dressed in less than a minute, craving that coffee and maybe even a cigarette, and sharply aware of just how hungry he'd become.

Tucking his shirttail into his jeans, he hurried down the hall, pausing at the muted sound of Nikki's voice coming from beyond the kitchen door. Suddenly, his cravings vanished. Even the headache seemed less intense when he imagined her making their breakfast, entertaining the sprout with nursery rhymes as she worked . . . and little Claire, hugging that old rag doll of hers, bouncing happily in her highchair. The image sparked a rush of confusion within him, warm anticipation . . . and unexpected dread. They shouldn't be here. What if he grew to care for them? What if it happened again?

A second voice, quiet but unmistakably male, startled him out of his reverie. So, Nikki had a man. Not surprising. Hadn't he told himself the woman wasn't as innocent as she seemed? He eased closer to the door, wishing he'd left it ajar last night instead of turning the key in the lock. Hell, it was none of his business. Still, he couldn't help wondering if she intended to make a habit of entertaining her boyfriends over breakfast.

'Lord help us, little Missy . . . you might'a' killed the man.'

'Aw, come on . . . don't give me that look. I didn't know what else to do.' Nikki tucked a wayward strand of hair behind her ear and scooped a spoonful of strained pears into Claire's mouth. 'There you go, little bird,' she said, laughing as the baby bounced, kicked and cooed, dribbling at least half of the fruit onto her already messy chin.

'Still an' all . . . a frying pan?'

Nikki studied her elderly visitor for a long moment, trying to decipher the somewhat cryptic expression taking shape on his tanned and deeply-lined face. Noble Bateman looked worried, she decided. Worried, and something more . . . something that sparked a sly twinkle in his eyes.

'Listen,' she said, suddenly feeling the need to defend her actions, 'for all I knew, *he* was the one with murder on his mind. I've never met him, y'know. And he's *nothing* like what I expected.'

Noble lifted one bushy eyebrow, then slowly lowered it again, as if he'd answered his own question. Maybe if she finished the whole story, he'd answer a few of hers, too.

'I heard a noise . . . and then he turned on the kitchen lights . . . I thought he was some drifter who'd broken in . . . a burglar.' *Or hired assassin.*

'I just kept thinking about what he might do to Claire . . . and then the power cut out, and he was standing there taking his wet clothes off, and . . . and . . . '

Nikki felt her cheeks grow uncomfortably warm as the suddenly vivid image of Gren Wilder, naked to the waist and about to shed his jeans, tangled the words on her tongue.

'Must'a shocked him terrible to find you and the little one here,' said Noble, obviously more interested in Gren's side of the story than her own. He stroked his salt-and-pepper moustache, a habit she'd come to associate with sober reflection on his part, then asked, 'What'd he say?'

'Not much. He just grumbled at me, finally said he'd give us a week.'

'Poor soul.'

'What? Noble!' Nikki shoveled another spoonful of pears into Claire's mouth, then glanced at her watch. Eight-fifteen. If she didn't get her answers soon, it'd be too late. 'Noble?'

she repeated, 'I think it's time you told me about Gren Wilder, don't you? I mean, what have Claire and I gotten ourselves into?'

The old man shook his head and sniffed. 'Such a sorrowful thing . . . fit to break your heart, little Missy. Happened nigh on six year ago, now. Awful. Terrible — awful.'

'Oh, for heaven's sake, Noble. He'll be out here looking for his breakfast any minute now. *Just tell me.* Please?'

'Well, was near Christmas time, if I recollect right. Our Gren was away somewheres, chasin' his stories. Never could understand why he'd stay away at Christmas . . . such a shame . . . '

'*Noble!*' She glared across the table at him and felt a twinge of regret as Noble's mouth wobbled open in an expression of utter astonishment. Small wonder. In eight months, she'd never once raised her voice to him. Until now. She drew a deep breath, curbing her impatience.

'I'm sorry, Noble. But if we're going

to stay here, in his house, I need to know some things.'

'Well, Miss Larssen, if you need to know something, perhaps you should just ask.'

Pity her back was turned, thought Gren, as he strode into the kitchen. He'd have to bet the expression on her face was worth at least a thousand words. Almost as good as his own must have been a moment ago, when he'd realized Nikki's 'man' was Noble Bateman. He refused to dwell on the sense of relief the realization had imparted.

'Aaaaaaaakk!' exclaimed Claire, waving a two-fisted greeting, then focusing her attention on the spoon in her mother's right hand. Laden with a whitish, mushy glop, it hovered midway between a half-full bowl of the stuff and the sprout's eagerly opened mouth. 'Aaaaaaaakk!' she squealed again.

Apparently the glop tasted a lot better than it looked.

Gren stepped closer, resting one

hand on the back of Nikki's chair. She didn't move a muscle, just sat there, ramrod-stiff, while the sprout thumped impatiently on her highchair.

Bending, he closed his hand around Nikki's, guiding the spoon home just in time to avoid another head-splitting shriek from Claire. 'Seems the young lady's hungry this morning, too,' he said, his hand lingering a moment longer than was really necessary. At such close range, Miss Larssen smelled incredibly good . . . like vanilla and cinnamon and . . . didn't she know how dangerous that could be around a hungry man?

Without thinking, Gren let his fingers trail along the inside of Nikki's wrist as he freed her hand. Her reaction left him puzzled . . . a slight, almost imperceptible tremble. Was she still afraid?

He looked up, caught Noble watching, and straightened abruptly. She was right to be afraid of him. The old man thought so, too. What else could that woebegone expression mean?

Suddenly self-conscious, Gren shoved both hands into the pockets of his jeans and turned his full attention to their visitor. 'Well, Noble. You're looking fit.'

Noble's frown gave way to a broad, welcoming grin that crinkled the corners of his eyes. 'As a fiddle, m'boy. And just lookit you . . . my, my, my . . . I'd hardly know you. Welcome. Welcome home, Gren-boy.'

For the second time this morning, it felt almost good to be home. Gren let himself relax. 'Good to see you, too, old man. You haven't changed a bit. Is that coffee I smell?'

Nikki glanced up, sending a brief flicker of smile his way. 'Mmmm-hmmm. Thought you might be in *need* of some this morning, Mr. Wilder.'

Touché. He let the sarcasm pass unchallenged. She'd be gone in a week, anyway. Let her think whatever she wanted. Unfortunately, it wasn't too hard to imagine what that might be. Something inside him demanded a little harmless revenge.

'About that coffee . . . ' He pressed a hand to her shoulder, certain the thought of serving him had never even occurred to her. 'Oh, please . . . don't get up. I'll get it myself.'

Ignoring the not-too-subtle reminder of her new place in the scheme of things at Wilder House, Nikki swiped a dribble of fruit off Claire's chin and loaded up the spoon again. How much of her conversation with Noble had Gren overheard? She struggled to remember exactly what had been said but, for some strange reason, found it difficult to think beyond the lingering warmth of Gren's touch on her hand, her wrist, and now her shoulder.

She studied the two men. Broad-shouldered and long-legged, they made her kitchen seem terribly small. And, judging from the way they were grinning at each other, they'd been a lot more than just neighbors all those years ago. She felt like a stranger at a family reunion.

Family reunion. No. She couldn't

afford to think about Lainey. Not now. The empty spoon slipped from her fingers, striking the table with a clatter as the suddenly vivid image of her sister's face crowded Nikki's mind. Vibrant and happy at first. Then, mirroring the nightmares, Lainey's laughter began to fade . . .

'Missy . . . ' Noble picked up the spoon, pressed it back into her hand and gave a gentle squeeze. 'You all right?'

'What? Oh, I . . . I'm fine.' She managed a weak smile, tried to steady her hand as her stomach lurched. This was *not* the time to think about Lainey. *Shut her out!* 'I'm fine,' she repeated. 'Just a bit tired . . . '

'My fault, Noble. Seems I kept our Miss Larssen up rather late last night.'

Nikki pinned her thoughts on Gren's voice, forced herself to focus on him until the image of her sister flickered and died. He was contemplating the clean and neatly folded laundry on the counter, and wearing a hard-to-read expression. Surprise, maybe, with a generous serving of guilt.

'It could have waited, you know.'

'I couldn't sleep.' *Not with you in the house. Not when I didn't know who you were, or what you wanted.*

The man studied her, silently questioning, and then smiled . . . as if he knew exactly what she'd left unsaid.

'Still taking care of business up at Ravensleigh, Noble?' His steady gaze never strayed from her face as he spoke. 'Or have you retired — like everyone else around here.'

The old man laughed, capturing Gren's attention at last, leaving Nikki to breathe a sigh of relief. What was it about him that kept her so on edge?

'Retire? What'd I do with m'self?'

Noble reached across the table as he spoke, tweaking the end of Claire's tiny nose, and laughing again when the baby crowed with delight. 'No, boy, I've outlived or outstayed three families up on that hill. Can't see as how they'd run the place without me.'

'Huh,' Gren chuckled. 'You're probably right about that.'

Nikki watched as he poured coffee and carried it back to the table. He didn't sit, choosing to lean against the old pine sideboard instead, just inches from her elbow. Crossing his legs at the ankles, he lifted the steaming mug to his lips. She didn't look up. Didn't have to. She could feel him watching again. What on earth did he want?

'Miss Larssen tells me you're having a party up at Ravensleigh today.'

'Pfffttt,' answered Noble. 'Not my doin'.' Turning back to Nikki, he reached under the bib of his overalls and pulled an envelope from the pocket of his faded green work shirt.

'From the lady. She says be sure to put a bug in yer ear 'bout her party. Wants everythin' there by three. I tell 'er Missus, our Nikki's never late. Not by a minute. But,' he rolled his eyes, lifting his shoulders in a shrug, as if to let the lady's barbed opinions roll off his back. 'Treats you shabby, she does.'

Sliding the envelope across the table, he continued, letting a mischievous smile twitch at the corners of his mouth. 'Figure I'll just take everythin' back with me this mornin', anyways. Save you the trip later. So, uh . . . did you make a little extra?'

'Don't I always?' Noble's grin was infectious and Nikki found herself beaming back at him. 'I fixed a special tray, just for you.'

'Ahhh, Missy. Never met nobody could fix up a supper as good as you. Ought'a be cookin' in some fancy restaurant down in Toronto. Not out here in the boonies feedin' rich folk who don't know how to appreciate 'ya.'

Nikki reached for the envelope — cash payment, as usual. And that, for the time being anyway, was all the appreciation she needed, or wanted, for 'feedin' rich folk'.

Breakfast at eight! Good grief, she was likely to get herself fired before the first day was over. She sprang to her feet, tucking the envelope into the pocket of her jeans as she darted across the room. How could she have forgotten the man's breakfast? 'You must be hungry, Gren — uh, Mr. Wilder.'

'Wasting away.'

Oh, perfect. A little sarcasm before breakfast. *Deep breath . . . count to ten . . . ignore it!*

'So . . . would you like some pancakes?' Satisfied with the pleasantly perky tone she'd managed to achieve, Nikki reached for a skillet. 'The batter's ready, and Noble brought some of his maple syrup.'

'Sounds good, but — '

Skillet in hand, she turned to find Gren gaping at her in mock horror.

'I'll be good,' he said, solemnly straight-faced. 'Just don't hit me again, okay?'

'Very funny.' Nikki sighed. Ignoring Gren Wilder was a whole lot easier said than done. Especially when he was right. She really should apologize for last night. But then, so should he. And something told her that wasn't too likely. 'So, um . . . how's your head this morning?'

Gren lifted one hand to his temple, his expression pained. 'I'll live. I suppose.'

Oh, boy. The man was really pushing his luck. And Noble, chuckling away to himself, was enjoying the show just a little too much. Nikki flashed her old friend a warning glance.

'Nothing a bit of breakfast wouldn't cure,' added Gren, favoring her with a grin. It was an unexpectedly boyish grin, lopsided and charming, and Nikki had the uncomfortable feeling she'd soon learn to hate it. Claire, however, seemed utterly delighted as he sank onto the chair and ladled a spoonful of fruit into her mouth.

'I was beginning to think I'd have to share Claire's bowl of glop,' he said, wiping her tiny chin as if he'd done it a hundred times before. 'Bet you wouldn't mind that at all, would you, Sprout?'

'Ga-ga!' Claire leaned forward to pat his face with sticky hands. Gren laughed.

Seemed the baby had found herself a walking, talking, Raggedy Man after all. Was this really the same miserable lout who'd blown into their lives on last night's storm? Astonishing as the transformation was, Noble's reaction to it was even more surprising. The old man sniffed loudly and wiped what might have been a tear from the corner of his eye, straightening abruptly when Gren shot him a threatening look. Whatever 'sorrowful story' the two of them were hiding, she intended to get to the bottom of it. Shouldn't be too hard. All she'd have to do was get Noble alone.

4

Gren rested his elbows on the desk, leaning as close to the open window as he dared. Nikki was only a few steps away, playing with Claire on the lawn. She hadn't yet realized she was being watched, and once she did the moment would be lost. She would close down, suspicious and weight-of-the-world serious, just as she'd been in the kitchen last night. For some strange reason, he wasn't ready for that.

Huh. What was it about her that kept him fascinated, glued to the window? He had work to do, articles to write, a book to be outlined. But here he sat. God help him, given the chance, he would probably watch her all day.

Her eyes . . . maybe they were at fault. Such incredible eyes, the color of new spring grass, not angry or suspicious as they'd been last night, but shining with a wordless expression of joy and unconditional love that left him aching with loneliness.

Or maybe it was the child in her arms, the lucky recipient of all that mother-love. Waving her tiny, dimpled hands in the air, the sprout squealed with delight, babbling away in a language only little girls and mothers could understand. A language he'd never expected to hear again. Not in Wilder House, anyway.

'Don't go!' His words spilled out in a hoarse whisper that surprised him every bit as much as they would have surprised Nikki, if she'd heard. No chance of that, though. She was halfway across the lawn already, slow-dancing with Claire in the dappled shade of the old Norway maple. Whatever happened to the swing he'd put up in that tree? It hadn't been anything special, just a board and a length of rope, but he'd made it himself . . .

It struck him like a fist in the gut — a fist that grabbed, and twisted, and drove the breath from his lungs. A memory so vivid he could almost touch it . . . almost. He pushed his chair back, stared for a painfully long moment at the desk drawer, then eased it slowly open, trying to ignore the tremor in his hands, the sudden quickening of his pulse as he reached inside. It was just a picture, after all. A relic . . . a part of his soul left face-down in the drawer. The very best part.

Carefully, lovingly, he lifted the small, burnished frame and placed it gently on the desktop. Gazing at the smiling faces of his wife and baby daughter for the first time in nearly six years, he felt his stomach wrench again. Oh, how he longed to hold them, to feel their warmth in his arms. So beautiful . . . so full of life and love. They were the ones who should be outside playing on the lawn, dancing in the shade, laughing . . . *living*. What gave Aprile the right to send strangers to take their place? What gave him the right to watch those strangers . . . and dream?

'Mr. Wilder?'

Gren snapped to attention and fixed his gaze on the window, expecting to meet Nikki's frosty glare beyond the screen. But she'd vanished. The yard was empty. How long had he been sitting there brooding? Remorse was a sly thief, he thought, stealing his life away by bits and pieces.

'Mr. Wilder?'

He turned to find her standing in the doorway, looking partially windblown and completely impatient. 'I'm trying to work, Miss Larssen. What is it?'

'Sorry, I — oooh — ow! Claire, sweetie, let go. That hurts Mommy!' Grimacing, she tried to coax the baby's tiny fist out of her hair. Gren resisted the urge to lend a hand, leaning back in his chair to watch the battle, instead. The sprout was one determined little bundle of energy, and Nikki hadn't really sounded 'sorry' at all.

'Sorry to bother you,' she repeated at last, tucking the rescued tangle of hair behind her ear before she continued.

'We'll be going to town in a while. Thought you might need something before we leave — some lunch or a fresh pot of coffee? Or maybe you'd like us to pick up a few things while we're out?' Settling Claire on her hip, she leaned back against the door jamb and waited. She was almost smiling.

Gren straightened abruptly, planting his feet firmly beneath his chair, trying to avoid meeting her gaze, and feeling distinctly uncomfortable. Pick up a few things? Despite all his snarling and sarcasm, the woman was honestly trying to make this ridiculous arrangement work. She'd done all that smelly laundry without so much as a single complaint, cooked an incredible breakfast — a bit late, but absolutely delicious — and now she was offering to run errands?

Of course. He let himself return the smile. That's what she was up to. The trip to town was just an excuse to visit Noble and finish her inquisition. Not that it would do her one bit of good.

He'd made certain of that this morning. Noble Bateman was nothing if not loyal. And while obviously very fond of Nikki, the old man's ties to the Wilder family ran deep. He wouldn't talk. As for Nikki, well, she'd be gone in a week, anyway. She didn't need to know. And he didn't need her pity. He'd had his fill from that bitter cup six years ago.

'Mr. Wilder?' Shifting restlessly from one foot to the other, Nikki hiked the sprout up to her shoulder and breathed a long-suffering sigh. Her expression suggested she thought he might have lost whatever was left of his mind.

'I've got everything I need right here,' he said, watching her gaze flicker briefly toward the half-empty bottle of Scotch on the desk. When she looked back, those sparkling, green eyes of hers seemed cold and unforgiving, made him want to explain himself, made him want to tell her he'd been on his way to the parlor to put the bottle away . . .

Damn! Why did he care what she thought? What he drank, and when, was none of her business. For an instant he wished he hadn't already flushed the last of his cigarettes. He'd have lit one up right then and there, just to spite her. Instead he muttered, 'Everything except a little privacy, that is.'

Nikki reacted as if she'd been slapped, hugging the baby a bit closer as she retreated into the hall. 'I'm very sorry. We won't bother you again.' She spoke briskly, efficiently, then hesitated as if something more needed to be said.

'*What?*'

'I should . . . that is, sometime when it's convenient for you . . . I really should clean up in here.'

She was right. The place was a mess. 'Don't bother.'

'It's no bother. I should've had everything ready, but your sister asked me to stay out — '

'My sister was right.' Blunt and to the point. Why didn't she take the hint?

'It must be terribly dusty after so long . . . '

'Everything was covered,' he muttered, nodding at the pile of white sheets in the corner.

'Yes, but — ' Whatever she'd been about to say, Nikki seemed to think better of it, giving a curt nod instead. 'Let me know if you change your mind.'

He wasn't sure what impulse brought him to his feet and sent him stalking out into the hallway after her. She was leaving, taking the sprout and getting out of his way. That was exactly what he wanted . . . wasn't it?

'Say hello to Noble for me,' he growled, regretting the harshly-spoken words the moment they left his mouth — even more so when Claire looked back at him, wide-eyed, and burst into tears. Nikki didn't bother to turn around, just pulled the kitchen door shut behind her as she passed through.

Gren sighed. What was she thinking about him? he wondered. What was she saying, right now, to comfort the sprout? He slouched into his chair, wishing he could take back most of the last ten minutes, wishing he could dry the baby's tears. He hadn't meant to frighten her, hadn't meant to antagonize her mother, either. But he'd done both, without even trying. It would be best for all of them if they did move on at the end of the week. Trouble was, according to Aprile, they had nowhere else to go. He glanced at the picture on the desk. His family. They'd left this house because of him, too. And now, because of him, they were dead.

★ ★ ★

He couldn't remember reaching for the whisky bottle, or finding the tarnished brass key in the bottom of the desk drawer, or even walking across the hall . . . but there he stood, staring bleakly at the door he thought he'd locked forever six long years ago. He fumbled with the key, fought to steady his hand and ease the pounding of his heart, felt his stomach lurch as the door swung slowly open. He'd left the blinds drawn all those years ago and now the nursery wore its darkness like a shroud.

Stale, dusty air chafed his lungs as he moved uneasily through the room, trailing his hand across the baby's dresser, the huddled collection of plush stuffed animals, the back of the Bentwood rocker — Becca's favorite place to nurse. He could almost see her there, smiling up at him, reaching out to touch his hand.

Stopping beside the crib, Gren rested his elbows on the rail as he had so many times before. Amy's butterfly mobile had gathered cobwebs over the years. It tinkled a few melancholy notes of Rockabye Baby as he reached to brush them away.

Time will ease the pain. His breath caught in his throat. What a lie that was. His pain, his guilt, would stay with him forever. He'd failed them, lost them, then tried to lose himself. But all he'd managed to lose was his reputation. He glanced down at the bottle in his left hand, remembering how he'd blown his last decent assignment because he'd been drunk all the time. Wound up bumming around the Middle East and Europe, filing stories that weren't worth his time or anyone else's, trashing what was left of his credibility. Until four weeks ago. He'd awakened from the nightmare, met the day sober for the first time in months, and he'd known it was time to come home.

He'd been certain he could talk his way into another chance with the paper, a new career, a future. Maybe he still could, if . . .

He lifted the bottle, sorely tempted to pull the cork. Last night had been the first drink in nearly a month. It would be so easy to slide back into old habits now. He could blame it all on a certain green-eyed beauty and her little angel — living, breathing reminders of all he'd lost. Except it wouldn't be their fault. It would be his fault. Just like always.

The bottle clattered against the wooden slats of the crib as he leaned closer, remembering how tiny his little girl had seemed the last time he'd held her, remembering her bright, blue eyes, so full of innocence and trust, her tiny pink fingers curling tight around his. She'd had dark hair, too, though not as dark as Claire's.

No more. Gren hurled the bottle, flinching when it shattered against the far wall, then brushing the back of his hand across his eyes. Why on earth was he crying now, after all these years? At the time, he hadn't been able.

Lifting a pale pink blanket out of the crib, he drew it close, brushed the soft folds across his cheek. It smelled of dust, but that was wrong. His memory of how it should smell was still so vivid . . . baby powder, sweet sunshine, just like his daughter. Just like Claire. He felt his knees buckle, heard the sob rise in his throat. It sounded so distant . . . as if it had come from someone else.

It was finally time. Time to let the tears fall, to wash away some of the grief and guilt, to numb the pain. And it was time to stop living in the past, to face the fact that he couldn't turn back the clock, couldn't bring back his family. But he *could* become a man his daughter would be proud of.

★ ★ ★

'Oh, no . . . *please*, no.' Nikki flinched at the sound of breaking glass, felt her heart stammer as she fixed her gaze on the door at the end of the kitchen. Claire shuddered, snuggling closer, still sound asleep and a dead weight in her arms.

If only they'd left for town right away, instead of stopping for juice and a comforting snuggle. Now she needed to run, to get out of the house, at least find a place to hide. But her feet wouldn't move. She could not get out of her chair. This wasn't supposed to happen again. Not to her. *Never* to Claire.

'I'll take care of you,' she murmured,

but the voice she heard was not her own. *I'll take care of you.* Lainey's words, Lainey's voice. *We're going to hide . . . he won't find us.*

She was five years old again, playing dolls on the floor with her big sister. They should have been in bed. Eight o'clock, every night. That was Carl's rule. And Mom always went by Carl's rules. They were lucky to have him she said. Lucky to have a roof over their heads and food on the table. *Lucky to have him.*

'Get under the bed!' Lainey grabbed her hand and pulled. 'He's gonna be mad, now. He's gonna come looking. Be quiet! Don't cry! Just get under the bed. *I'll take care of you. I promise.*'

Lainey had never been able to keep that promise. She hadn't even managed to take care of herself. So now it was all up to Nikki. Repeating her sister's words — loudly, to make herself believe — she pushed herself out of the chair. She would not let it happen again. 'I'll take care of you, Claire. I promise.'

⋆   ⋆   ⋆

'Tell me the truth, Noble. *The truth*. Not what *he* told you to say.'

Interrupting the game of 'horsy' he and Claire were playing, the old man turned to stare at Nikki, his grey eyes as sharp as the edge in his voice. 'Now you hear this, little Missy — nobody tells Noble Bateman what to say. Not Gren Wilder, nor nobody else.'

'Then why — '

'Missy, the truth of it is, he asked me not to say. It's his privacy I'm tryin' to respect. Same as your'n. Didn't you ask me not to pry? Eh? And don't be tellin' me it's different. Ain't no difference at all. You got secrets in your past, Missy. We both knows it. Well, so's your Gren. And he's the one who'll tell 'em. When he's ready.'

Nodding abruptly, Noble set his knee in motion again, a signal that, for him at least, the discussion had come to an end. Claire giggled and waved her arms in the air. Not a care in the world. If only life were so simple.

Nikki smiled as she watched them at play, touched by the genuine affection she saw in Noble's eyes. So much more was at stake than just a place to stay. This man was as close to a father figure as she could ever hope to have. And she did trust him — or always had, until now. But this was one gigantic leap of faith he wanted. How could she make him understand?

'I'm afraid to stay there, Noble. He's so angry.'

'Didn't seem so angry this mornin', smilin' at the wee one the way he was.' Noble glanced up at her again, as if daring her to deny it. 'Pretty impressed with your breakfast, too, I recollect.'

'But after you left, he . . . ' She hesitated. It all seemed so foggy, now. Had she imagined it? The man did have work to do, after all. And they *had* interrupted him. Wasn't it possible he'd knocked that bottle off the corner of his desk by accident?

'He did what, Missy?' Noble had

stopped bouncing again and studied her, grim-faced.

'Just shut himself up in his office. And when I asked if he needed anything from town, he . . . he looked so strange. And then he got mad. He made Claire cry, and he . . . I think he threw a bottle — smashed it against the wall.' Or maybe it fell. No. She couldn't afford to take that chance. She had to be sure.

'Noble, what if you're wrong? What if he goes from hurling bottles to hurting Claire?'

He laughed. It was obviously a thought that had never occurred to him and he didn't give it a moment's notice now. 'You trust me, Missy?'

'You know I do.'

'Then trust this. Gren won't hurt you. Or the little one. He'd take himself away again b'fore he'd let that happen. *Believe it.*'

Noble bounced Claire off his knee, swinging her into Nikki's arms with the strength and ease of a man half his age.

'Best get myself back to that party, before the lady comes a-lookin'.' Resting his hand on her shoulder, he gave an encouraging squeeze. 'Give him a chance, little Missy. You won't be sorry.'

5

'You have every right to be here,' she told herself, saying the words aloud to give them a little weight, an air of truth. They struck the silence like a challenge. Nikki shot a nervous, backwards glance down the hallway. Cleaning was part of her job, wasn't it? She was cleaning. So what was the big problem?

The floorboards creaked underfoot. It was more of a groan, really, a warning. *Keep out.* She twisted the knob, let the door swing slowly open and, with one last look over her shoulder, slipped into Gren's private study.

If ever a room suited its owner, this was it, she thought, tucking the duster into the pocket of her jeans. The place was as much a puzzle as the man himself. How did he ever find anything?

The walls, or what she could see of

them, were the same nicotine-yellow as the stucco ceiling, explaining the gone-but-not-forgotten odor of stale cigarette smoke. A folding table, its top cluttered with files, newspaper clippings, and aging magazines took up most of one corner, standing guard over a collection of cardboard file boxes — no labels, just dates. The last had been shoved beneath the table six years ago.

Overflowing bookshelves lined the walls and she scanned the titles, wondering if Gren had actually read the entire collection. Steinbeck, Zola, Price. And open on the floor, the poems of John Donne. It seemed, wherever she turned, there were a lot more questions than answers about Gren Wilder.

She'd spotted him on her way back from Vinegar Hill, ploughing through one of Mr. Beckett's cow pastures, head down, hands shoved deep into his pockets. Walking off his anger? Or working up another rage?

Gren won't hurt you. Or the little

one. He'd take himself away again b'fore he'd let that happen. Believe it.

'Prove it,' muttered Nikki. There had to be something in this house, in this room, that would shed a little light on the man. Although what compelled her to search for that 'something' was beyond her. She ought to be upstairs packing instead of snooping around in his private space.

Stepping quickly back to the door, she listened for one long moment to the silence of the empty house — expectant, as if it, too, were waiting for something to happen. From the nursery monitor, clipped to her belt, came a soft rustling sound, like leaves in the wind, as Claire shifted in her sleep. Suddenly, her compulsion was very clear. The baby was at home here. And safe. From everything but Gren Wilder, that is. Proof, or at least some hint of an explanation for his erratic behavior, was the only thing that would set her mind at ease.

She crossed the room, stopping in

front of his desk. It was old oak, dark and heavy looking. The tapes she'd found in his duffel bag last night littered the top, spilled onto the floor. She flipped through the notebooks he'd left front and center — nothing but blank pages. Maybe the man had writer's block. That would explain the mood swings . . . wouldn't it?

Her gaze fell to the slightly ajar desk drawer, and the splash of color within. The drawer resisted, screeched a complaint as she tugged it open. *Keep out.* She glanced over her shoulder again, then reached for the portrait Gren had hidden away.

The woman and child in the picture were laughing, happy . . . both obviously much in love with whomever held the camera. Who were they? she wondered. Their clothes were modern, the color crisp and sharp, so it couldn't be his mother and sister. Then who? His wife? His lover? His child? Nikki stared at the smiling faces.

Such a sorrowful thing . . . fit to

break your heart.

Turning, she gazed across the room, across the hallway, at the locked door opposite Gren's study.

Happened nigh on six year ago, now. Awful. Terrible-awful.

His family? The picture drew her gaze again, but instead of the smiling woman and child, Nikki found herself staring at her own reflection in the polished glass. Momentarily startled, she looked away. She usually avoided mirrors — harsh reminders of her new reality, her new identity. She looked again and frowned. It was time to touch up the hair. The black was beginning to fade, letting hints of her natural reddish-brown shine through. She made a face, doubtful she'd ever get used to it. But short black hair was part of the act. The most important part. It made her look like Claire, kept people from wondering. No one would ever guess. They looked almost as much like mother and daughter as the woman and child in Gren's photo.

Gently, she returned the portrait to the drawer, feeling more guilty than curious all of a sudden. Until she saw the key. Would it open the door? Did she dare try? She chewed on her lip. Gren would be back soon. If she wanted answers, she'd have to take her chance. Now. It might be the only chance she'd have.

Pushing guilt to the back of her mind, she hurried across the hall, hiding the stolen key in the palm of her hand. It slipped easily into the lock. As the door swung open, the mellow, bittersweet aroma of old whisky spilled over her. This was where it had happened. Something beyond this door had driven Gren Wilder into a bottle-smashing rage. Half afraid of what she might find inside, Nikki groped around the corner for the light switch. It made a hollow click. The room stayed dark. Heart pounding, she stepped cautiously through the door.

Not what she'd expected — although she wasn't entirely certain what she'd expected. But not this. Not a tiny, empty crib, a rocking chair, a crumpled pink blanket on the floor, and an almost overwhelming sense of sadness. She bent to pick up the blanket.

'What are you doing?'

Gren's voice sounded flat, emotion-less — a tired question, not a threat. Even so, she found herself backing away from him, nervously clutching the blanket to her breast.

'I — ' The words caught in her throat. How had he managed to sneak up on her without so much as a squeak from the screen door in the kitchen? He filled the doorway now, blocking escape, his face shrouded in shadow. She took another step back, carefully folding the pink blanket, smoothing it between her hands. When she draped it over the crib rail, Gren turned away, breathing a sigh that shuddered through the room — through her. And she knew. It wasn't rage he was feeling, but grief. He crossed the hallway and slouched into his chair, back to the door.

'I'm so sorry,' murmured Nikki, watching as he raked the fingers of both hands through his blond, wind-tangled hair. 'So very sorry.'

Suddenly it all made sense. His anger, his aloofness, his fascination with Claire . . . it was all about his family. What could have happened to them?

Quietly she gathered the shards of broken glass, mopped up the spilled whisky and wiped the wall and floor. When she was finished, she paused at the door to Gren's study. He still hadn't moved. 'Are you all right?'

His shoulders stiffened at the sound of her voice, but he didn't reply.

'I shouldn't have . . . that is . . . it's just — ' No. Now was not the time for explanations. *Leave the man alone.* 'I'm sorry I intruded.'

'Wait.'

His voice had a huskiness to it that tugged at her heart, pulled her back to the doorway. She waited.

'I'm the one who should apologize.'

101

He sighed again as he turned to face her, meeting her gaze, calm and steady. A little too calm, she thought. Almost numb. His face was deathly pale, his dark eyes glistened.

'I should've told you,' he said flatly. 'Or Aprile should have. It isn't right.'

'I know. We shouldn't be here.'

'That's not what I meant. It's ... Nikki, this house is so full of sadness ... always has been.'

She shook her head. 'We've been happy here, Gren.'

'Happy?' He stared blankly into the space between them. 'But ... they're dead.' His words hung in the air, an almost visible plea.

Nikki stepped into the room, feeling awkward and helpless, uncertain of what to do next. Should she sit? Let him know she was ready to listen? But Gren had the only chair. Sinking cross-legged onto the floor, she looked up and found him still staring into space, strangely unfocused. 'What happened?'

'My fault . . . ' he murmured, after a long, heavy silence. 'Amy . . . she was just a baby . . . just Claire's age . . . it would've been her first Christmas.'

His voice cracked. Nikki touched the hem of his jeans, then pulled away, afraid to intrude again, unwilling to end his moment of truth.

'My fault,' he repeated, brushing the back of his hand across his eyes.

Oh, God . . . was he going to cry? What was she supposed to do then? She could feel him withdrawing as she watched, reliving his past. No tears fell, but when he spoke again his voice was taut with emotion.

'I shouldn't have gone. But Becca, my wife . . . she said they'd be fine. 'Go,' she said. 'It's a big story. *Really big*.' Y'know, I can't even remember which story it was, now.'

Resting his elbows on his knees, Gren cradled his head in his hands. 'It was supposed to be a surprise. Christmas in Panama City. Together. Becca had it all planned. I . . . I didn't know.'

He faltered, retreating into silence that, for Nikki, was every bit as eloquent as words.

'Gren?' She moved closer, rising to her knees in front of him and gently touching his shoulder. Tracing a knot of muscle with her fingers, she let her hand drift gently down his arm, felt him shudder and tense at the unexpected contact. Suddenly she longed to do more, to wrap her arms around him, comfort him, urge him to trust her . . . but how could she? Trust was a two way street . . . a road she had no right to travel.

As if he sensed her hesitation Gren slowly raised his head, meeting her gaze with eyes so full of sorrow, she feared her heart might break.

'I should've known,' he said softly. 'Always said it would be different for us . . . but I turned out just like him, didn't I?'

'Just like . . . what are you talking about? Just like who?'

He managed a wry smile. 'The

writer. Your boring, stuffy old man.' His voice grew cold. 'My father.'

Nikki rocked back on her heels, let her hand fall away from his arm. She knew that tone of voice and it scared her.

'Work always came first. We grew up without him, Aprile and me. And I swore that would never happen to my family. Not to Amy.'

Suddenly Gren thrust the chair back, putting a couple of feet of space between them. She could sense what he was feeling, the anger, the frustration. A frightening combination. She pushed to her feet, watching him uneasily.

'The story was hot, y'know ... *I couldn't just leave ...* '

His voice cracked again as he searched her face, her eyes. What was he looking for? she wondered. Understanding? Forgiveness? But it wasn't her place to forgive him. He was going to have to do that for himself. 'Gren, you — '

'No.' It was more of a groan than a

word. 'Becca said she understood . . . I didn't know she'd try to come to me . . . they . . . their plane went down . . . I . . . '

He stared at her, then shook his head, hard, as if to shake off the memories. 'Huh. How's that for more than you wanted to know?' Before she could answer, he added softly, 'More than I wanted to tell, too.'

'I don't mind. Really.' Feeling suddenly awkward and out of place, not to mention way out of her element, Nikki tried to look away, but something in his expression kept her focused on his face. 'It helps sometimes . . . to talk, I mean.'

'Yeah, right.' His smile flickered, bittersweet and painfully brief, and she knew the irony of her words wasn't lost on him. Parking the chair in front of his desk again, he flipped open one of the notebooks and picked up a pencil. 'Guess I owe you one then.'

Nikki stared at his back, broad shoulders beneath a worn blue cotton shirt. *I owe you one.* Did he know how she longed to let him make good on that debt? It would be such a relief to finally tell someone . . . to trust someone . . .

Turning, she left him alone in the room.

★   ★   ★

It was time to move on, anyway. Past time. Dangerous to stay in one place too long, letting people get to know you, making friends, relying on them — losing your edge. 'Way past time to move on.' Nikki looked up from the row of cherry tarts she was capping and met Claire's gaze across the kitchen table. 'Right pumpkin?'

Claire flattened her own lump of pie dough with an open-handed smack and gave Nikki a very wet raspberry. 'Pllllltt!'

Nikki laughed. 'Was that an opinion?'

Claire was too busy smacking the dough to pay attention. Well, pretty good opinion, if that's what it was. They were really going to miss this place. And Noble. *Especially* Noble. The smart thing would be to leave without telling him anything. What he didn't know couldn't hurt him, after all. But what if he got worried, called in the police? No. Any report about a missing woman and child, even in a half-horse town the size of Vinegar Hill, would be certain to bring Frank Medici running. And what Frank wanted to know *could* hurt Noble. It could hurt Gren, too.

No, she'd have to come up with a good reason, a completely believable story. Tie up all the loose ends, and then disappear — all in just six days.

She brushed the back of her hand across her face and studied the big, bright kitchen. She'd miss it most of all. Claire smacked the table again and laughed, drawing Nikki's attention. This was going to be terribly hard on the baby. Who knew how long they'd be on the run? Living in the back of the van . . . homeless . . . no kind of life for a child. No kind of life for anyone.

She sighed, letting herself remember, just for an instant, all the things that might have been. It sure wasn't supposed to be like this. She should've been in Paris now, apprenticed to one of the top chefs in Europe. But instead . . .

Claire looked up at her, hands full of pie dough, and smiled. A smile that lit up the room, and Nikki's heart. Suddenly, Paris didn't matter. Nothing mattered, except keeping Claire safe. A worthwhile goal for one lifetime . . . and one she wouldn't dare entrust to anyone else.

Enough! Shaking off the melancholy, Nikki carried the trays of tarts to the oven and slipped them inside. If they tasted even half as good as they looked, the *Minute Meals* folks were going to be smiling this week.

She glanced at the clock. It was six forty-five and Gren expected his dinner at seven. Nikki turned up the heat under the asparagus, gave the hollandaise a quick stir, and tested the chicken breasts with a fork.

'Something smells good.'

He strode into the room, looking nervous, awkward, as if he didn't know what to do with himself or his hands. Finally, he shoved them into his pockets and winked at Claire. 'Hey, sprout. What'cha doin'?'

To Nikki's surprise the baby just stared at him, her bottom lip curled into a pout. Was she remembering how he'd growled at them before . . . how frightened she'd been? Gren's smile was fading fast.

'We were making tarts . . . Claire's a terrific dough smasher. Right Claire? Dinner's almost ready — are you hungry?'

He didn't answer, just sat at the end of the table, as far away from the baby as he could possibly get. Nikki tried to avoid looking at him as she wiped the table and set out their dinner dishes, but it was almost impossible. She could feel him watching, his steady gaze following her back and forth across the room, his expression utterly dismal. He was probably wishing he hadn't promised a week, trying to think of a way to get them out of his house tonight.

Neither one of them spoke again until their dinner was on the table and Gren had tasted everything on his plate. So far, so good. His bleak expression was unchanged, but at least he hadn't gagged on anything. Yet. She took a deep breath. It was time to put the man out of his misery. 'Listen, I've been thinking — '

'Nikki, I — '

'Er . . . sorry. What were you going to say?'

He shook his head. 'It'll keep. You go ahead.'

Oh, no. No way. He was about to ask her to leave. She was certain of it. And if he did, there'd be one less lie she'd have to tell Noble. She gulped a mouthful of water. 'Please . . . I interrupted. You first.'

'It . . . it's this week thing,' he said

111

quietly, resting his fork on the edge of his plate. 'I think . . . I may have made a mistake . . . '

He picked up the fork, moved the food around his plate, finally looked up at her again. 'This is very good . . . really excellent.' Working up a half-hearted smile, he continued. 'Aprile was right. You're a wonderful cook.'

Hmmmm. Nice technique. 'Boy, this is great — oh, by the way, you're fired.' Why didn't he just come right out and say so? Maybe if she gave him a bit of help. 'I'm glad you like it . . . and I do understand, really.'

'Understand . . . ?' He dropped the fork again and stared across the table at her.

'Yes. About the week thing.'

He frowned.

Good grief, now what? Instead of relieved, the man looked monumentally confused — even more so after sneaking a quick peek at Claire, who was smashing a lump of pie dough on Raggedy Man's face. Had Gren made the 'Ga-ga' connection, too?

He winced.

Apparently so. And apparently she was going to have to carry the conversation. 'We'll need at least a couple of days to get organized . . . I have customers to contact and *Minute Meals* to deliver . . . but don't worry, we'll be out of your way before the week's up.'

'A couple of days? But — '

'Surely that's not too much to ask!' Good grief, did he really want them out tonight? Maybe Claire had the right idea. It was just too darned bad that the rest of the dough was baking in the oven.

'It's not — '

'This has been home for eight months, Mr. Wilder. You can't honestly expect — '

'Nikki . . . '

' — us to pack up, find a new place, and close down a business overnight.'

'Of course not.'

'I mean, surely . . . ' She met his

gaze. He didn't look quite so confused anymore. 'What did you say?'

'Think you might let me finish this time?'

Claire thumped a little harder.

'Uh . . . sorry. Go right ahead.'

He took a deep breath. 'I think you should stay.'

'You . . . What?'

'Well, like you said, it's your home now, too. You've got the business going . . . ' He shrugged. 'What can I say? My sister was right this time. The food's great. The house is spotless. And the sprout . . . well, she's no bother at all. I hardly know the two of you are here when I'm back in the office. And we . . . that is, I . . . '

Nikki tried, a bit too late, to adjust her expression, settling somewhere between surprise and confusion, but Gren hadn't missed her initial, astonished reaction. He looked suddenly embarrassed, as if afraid he'd gone too far.

'Anyway,' he finished, almost gruffly,

'it'd be way too much trouble to find somebody else.'

Too much trouble? 'I see.' She took a long moment to study him. After all he'd been through, sharing his home with them had to hurt — a constant, painful reminder. He was probably hoping she'd refuse. *Of course.* He felt obligated, afraid something might happen if he sent them away. Ready to blame himself again. 'To tell you the truth, Gren, I've already decided to leave. It's probably best for everyone, don't you think? I mean — '

His suddenly wounded expression tangled the words on her tongue. She glanced across the table at Claire. Were they ganging up on her now? The baby's wide-eyed and woeful face was almost a mirror image of Gren's. But Claire couldn't possibly understand what was going on. Could she? Of course not.

The baby's bottom lip began to tremble.

'What's the matter, pumpkin?' she

asked, rounding the table to scoop Claire into her arms.

'She doesn't want to go,' said Gren, as if the answer were obvious.

The truth, of course, was that Claire was tired, her lump of dough had rolled under the table, and Raggedy Man's face was a sticky mess. Still, Gren's offer was tempting. And if Claire could make a choice, Nikki was certain that choice would be to stay right here at Wilder House. She hugged the baby a little closer. *It's your home now, too.* Well, he was right about that.

No taking chances this time, though. She'd make a plan, be ready to go when he started throwing things again. *If* he started throwing things again.

He was picking at his food now, trying to watch without being obvious, patiently waiting for her to decide. Patient but nervous, that is. Suddenly, she found it almost impossible to imagine him throwing things. She let herself smile. No point in making it too easy on him though. A little taste of his own medicine might be just what he needed right about now.

'All right, Mr. Wilder. If you're sure . . . maybe we'll give *you* a week.'

6

Gren hesitated at the bottom of the darkened stairway, hand on the railing, one foot poised above the first tread. He hadn't imagined it. Not the sprout after all, but her mother. It came again. A breathless, frightened cry that set his nerves on edge. Nightmare? Or . . .

Things had been tense between them after dinner. Nikki had been wary, studying him when she thought he wasn't looking, as if trying to figure out what his next move might be. Good trick if she could do it, seeing as he wasn't certain himself. He wondered, briefly, what she'd decided.

In any case, she wasn't likely to be too pleased about him barging into her room. Nightmare or not. But what if something was really wrong? What if she needed help?

Gren took the steps three to a stride.

The old staircase groaned, shattering the midnight silence, drowning out Nikki's sobs. At the top, he paused to turn on the light.

All doors but one stood open and from beyond that single door came another muffled sob. He moved quickly across the hall and stopped, resting his hand on the doorknob. What on earth had made her choose this room? The smallest of the lot. And why were the two of them sharing, when they could've had their pick — used all four of them for all he cared.

Suddenly, Gren remembered the expression he'd seen on Nikki's face that first night in the kitchen. The way she'd held the baby, so close to her heart and half-turned away from him, as if to shield the child from . . . from what? What was she so afraid of?

A faint rustling came from beyond the door and the crying stopped abruptly. Should he knock? Make sure she was okay? Bad idea. She'd be embarrassed, probably offended, *definitely* angry. Not a woman who needed or wanted a protector. He backed slowly away and eased himself down the stairs, silently cursing every creak and groan of old wood.

What did it matter if she knew he'd been checking up on her? It wasn't exactly a sin to show some concern over somebody else's distress, was it? But try as he might, he could only imagine her angry, letting him know in no uncertain terms that her nightmares were none of his business.

Gren poured himself some coffee, took one gulp and made a face. It was nearly as cold as Nikki's imagined voice. Leaving the half-full mug on the counter, he retreated to his study. Her dreams might be none of his business, but he was more convinced than ever that Nikki Larssen was keeping secrets. And more determined than ever to discover the truth.

★   ★   ★

Huddled on the edge of her bed, Nikki clutched a pillow to her breast and tried to stop the trembling. Through a haze of tears, she watched as Gren's shadow drifted across the thin line of light that crept beneath the door. She held her breath when the doorknob wobbled beneath his touch. He was listening. She could almost hear him breathing . . . whispering something.

Part of her wished he'd turn the knob and come in. One word from her and he'd be there, offering comfort, folding her safe in his arms. One word . . . *Gren*. Instead, she offered up a silent prayer that he'd leave her alone. He had to. She'd never survive the warmth of his body, the whisper of his breath in her hair, the brush of his lips against hers . . . Not now. She wasn't strong enough. Her life, her lies . . . it would all come undone.

Finally, the shadow moved and slowly withdrew. She didn't relax her hold on the pillow until he was halfway down the stairs, when that noisy step, fifth from the bottom, squealed under-foot. Then her breath shuddered out in a ragged sigh. How much had he heard?

Her heart raced as she sifted through the myriad possibilities. That dream again. Why now? What if she'd said something . . . Still shaky, she pushed to her feet and paced the room, stopping beside the crib when Claire whimpered in her sleep. 'Shhhhh, it's okay, pumpkin. I'm right here. You're safe . . . I promise.'

She moved to the window and stopped to listen, shivering as the cool night breeze stirred the heavy curtains. The house and everything beyond was eerily quiet. Not even a cricket's chirp. Just the low, haunted call of a freight train passing on the far side of town. The mournful sound always reminded her of home . . . the old steam clock in Gastown . . . every quarter hour . . .

Suddenly cold, she fell back onto the cot, wrapping herself in a blanket and curling her arms around her knees. She closed her eyes.

Gastown. It had been nearly nine months since the last time she'd heard that steam clock. An eternity. She'd felt cold then, too. A drizzly, December-in-Vancouver kind of cold that numbed her fingers and toes on the long walk home. And she'd been so tired. Double shifts at the restaurant always left her beat. All she wanted to do was crawl into bed and sleep. For at least a week.

She knew the instant she opened the door that someone had been there. The place felt different somehow . . . and not empty.

'Who's there?'

No answer.

She left the door ajar, hitting the switch to turn on the lights. Everything looked fine, just as she'd left it, but . . .

No. She was imagining things. Too much coffee and not enough sleep. She closed the door, fastened the chain, and kicked off her shoes. Trailing coat, scarf, and gloves on the floor in her wake, she made her way to the bedroom at the end of the hall. And froze.

She hadn't imagined anything. Somebody had been in the apartment and they'd left something behind — a dark, ominous something, resting in the center of her bed. Silence seemed to press in around her. She forced herself to take a deep breath and felt the blood tingle in her fingers and toes as her heart thudded back into action. She wanted to run, but her feet weren't going anywhere.

Be logical. Nobody else had a key. She hadn't expected any deliveries . . . and if the superintendent had let someone in with a package . . . why the bedroom?

Suddenly aware of a faint but plaintive sound, she crept closer to the bed. Whatever it was, it couldn't be alive . . . could it? Of course! Chef Winston. That cat of his had just had all those kittens.

Great. The guys in the kitchen were probably having a good laugh right about now. At her expense. *Just great.* What was she supposed to do with a box full of kittens? And how'd they ever gotten past the super, anyway? This was a strictly 'no pets' building.

Groaning, she hit the light switch, her mind on what was going to hit the fan in the morning. They weren't going to get away with —

The thought vanished. Breath caught in her throat as she stared down at the small form swaddled in blankets. The box wasn't really a box at all. It was a baby's travel bed. And that was no kitten.

Wrinkling its face, the child gave a soft, impatient cry and opened its eyes. The cry became a howl.

'Shhhhh.' She stared at the infant, the tiniest human being she'd ever seen, waving little fists in the air, feet flailing beneath the blanket, its face, so peaceful just seconds ago, now red and wrinkled. A wriggling mass of baby frustration. 'Shhhhh,' she repeated, resting her hand on the child's stomach, feeling utterly helpless, totally useless, and sorely tempted to shed a few tears of her own.

This couldn't be happening. What kind of monster abandoned a baby to a stranger? It had to be a mistake — a horrible mistake. A mix-up with apartment numbers, maybe. Even so, leaving the child alone for who-knew-how-long went far beyond bad judgement. It was unbelievable . . . and unforgivable. What the heck was she supposed to do about it? If only it would stop crying, give her just a minute to think . . .

'Shhhh . . . It's okay little one . . . ' She tried, not quite successfully, to steady her voice and control the trembling of her hands. The situation called for calm, rational thought, not panic. But panic was exactly what she felt . . . bubbling up inside of her, an irresistible force.

As the howl grew louder, her mental chaos gave way to instinct. She picked the child up, snuggling it close, whispering gentle reassurances, and wishing to heaven that someone would show up to reassure her.

She paced the room, swaying gently. Call the police. No. Call Social Services . . . get help from someone who actually had a clue what to do with a practically newborn baby.

Amazingly, after one or two more shuddering sobs, the baby stopped crying. It clung to her, kneading and nuzzling the front of her shirt, uttering soft, impatient little grunts and gurgles. Hungry.

'Sorry, kiddo, but you're out of luck in that department. Who brought you here, anyway? Did they leave you a bottle?'

Cradling the tiny person in one arm, she flipped back the blankets in the bassinet. No bottle. Just a piece of blue paper that fluttered out onto the bed.

As she reached to pick it up, the child in her arms began to whimper again. 'Shhhhh, shhhhh. It's okay. Just let me . . . '

Cat, the note began, in a spidery, rushed-looking script.

She sank onto the edge of the bed,

rocking gently. But her mind raced. Lainey was the only one who'd ever called her Cat. And only when she wanted something.

She's named after you. And you were right. But then, you always were the smart one. Remember how Mom used to say that? Smart and sensible.

Take care of her for me, okay? I'll come back, I promise. I just need some time to figure things out. Lainey.

She'd read the letter so many times in the past nine months she could almost see it, word-for-word, without ever bothering to unfold the blue paper. She supposed she'd known all along that Lainey wouldn't really come back. But she'd believed it for a while. Even Lainey had believed. For nearly two days. Until the phone call.

'No . . . ' Nikki hugged herself a little tighter, drew her knees up closer to her chest. She couldn't go through it again. Not now.

It's too late for me. But, Cat, I can't

let him hurt my baby.

'Please, Lainey . . . not now.' Her stomach twisted. A tight, impossible knot.

You were right about Frank . . . I should've listened.

'You never listened. *Never.*' Nikki buried her face in the pillow.

Too late for me. I'm already dead. It's all up to you.

★ ★ ★

'Rough night?'

Impatiently brushing a knot of hair away from her eyes, Nikki shot a quick glance in Gren's direction. Seemed the man had a talent for spotting the painfully obvious. What gave it away? she wondered. The bloodshot eyes? Maybe the dark circles underneath? Or the hair? Definitely the hair. Total bedhead.

He didn't look up. Just sipped his coffee and studied his newspaper. Fine. Be that way.

'Not particularly. Why?'

Idiot! Instead of heading him off, she'd just given him the perfect opener. She braced herself. Questions about last night, about what he'd heard, were inevitable. It was the answers that had her worried.

'No reason. I, um . . . I made coffee.' He gestured to the pot on the table, finally meeting her gaze. 'And you look like you could use some.'

'Oh, yeah? Well — ' She bit back the caustic reply. He was right. And trying very hard to be pleasant. If only he'd stop staring at her. She forced a smile. 'Guess I could use a cup. With sugar, please. And cream.'

She turned her back, depositing Claire in her highchair. Or trying to. Claire wasn't having any part of it. After eleven straight hours of sleep, she was wide awake and lively. A bundle of pure energy, looking for a little undivided attention. Make that a lot of undivided attention. Arms and legs flailing, the baby howled the one almost-word in her personal vocabulary. 'Na-na-na-nooo!'

'Here.' Gren appeared at Nikki's side, lifting the baby into his arms before she could object. 'Let me,' he said softly. 'Looks like the sprout's in the mood for some action before breakfast. Go drink your coffee.'

'But, I — '

'Relax.'

Relax? What the heck was that? It had been so long, she'd almost forgotten the meaning of the word.

'What d'ya say, Sprout? Shall we take a walk? Let your Mom have her coffee in peace?'

Claire pressed his face between her tiny hands and cooed happily as he strode toward the door. 'Ga-ga!'

'Wait!' Nikki caught his sleeve, pulling him back, fighting a nameless panic. 'You can't — '

'Hey.' His voice was steady, reassuring. 'I've been a father, remember?' She watched as his smile slowly faded. 'Not a very good one . . . but I do remember

131

how to work off a case of the morning jitters. Okay?' He hooked a chair with his foot and pulled it away from the table. 'Sit. We'll be back in twenty minutes.'

She opened her mouth, ready to object, but the somber expression on his face froze the words on her tongue.

'Good grief, Nikki,' he finished, meeting her gaze straight-on. 'How long has it been since you had a break?'

Nikki sank onto the chair as the screen door slammed shut behind them. 'Eight months, twenty-six days, and seventeen hours . . . give-or-take,' she whispered, swiping away the tears that stung her eyes. It was so unlike her to cry. Made her feel helpless and weak. Two things she'd sworn she would never be. Of course, she'd also sworn she'd never depend on a man to make things right. Claire's hoots of laughter drew her gaze to the window. And there he was. Making everything right. For Claire, anyway.

She gulped a mouthful of coffee. Two

days with Gren Wilder and here she sat, falling slowly apart, letting herself dream about his arms around her in the night. Letting him take control. This was *never* going to work.

★ ★ ★

'Breakfast is ready,' said Nikki, snatching the baby from his arms the moment he stepped through the kitchen door.

'You had fun,' she crooned, kissing Claire on the cheek. 'Oh, yes you did . . . I heard you laughing.'

The sprout laughed again as Nikki settled her, easily this time, into the highchair. 'Thanks,' she continued, sparing Gren the briefest of glances. 'Your breakfast is nearly ready, too. Just give me a minute.'

Turning, she swirled a spoon in a bowl of something he vaguely recognized as pablum, while Claire thumped eagerly on her tray. Apparently the woman didn't know how to take a break. One more try.

'I could do that for you, if — '

'*No!* I mean . . . thank you, but you've done enough. And anyway, this is our time.'

Gren eased into a chair and poured himself a second cup of coffee. Our time? From what he'd seen in the last two days, every waking minute was 'our time'. And they didn't even take a break to sleep alone. 'What smells so good?'

'Rhubarb muffins,' answered Nikki, wiping the sprout's chin with the corner of a teddy bear bib. 'They'll be done in another . . . ' She glanced at the timer on the stove. 'Two minutes.'

'Why did you do that?'

'Do what?' she asked quietly, not bothering to look at him.

'You know what. You were supposed to relax, not go on a baking spree.'

'What's the problem? You don't like rhubarb?'

'I don't like to see you running yourself ragged.'

Uh-oh! He shouldn't have said that. The woman's shoulders had stiffened

134

before the words were even out of his mouth.

'I made breakfast, Mr. Wilder. It's my job, remember?'

'Yes, but . . .'

'*But, what?*' This time, she turned as she spoke and glared at him across the table, her eyes so red and swollen, he had to wonder if she'd cried all night. And now she was practically daring him to admit he knew. His reporter's instincts told him there'd never be a better time to do a little digging. Take advantage of the moment. But another, older instinct wanted only to comfort her, maybe take a little comfort in return.

Her eyes narrowed. '*Well?*'

Resting his head in his hands, Gren winced as his fingers brushed the still-tender reminder of Nikki Larssen's preferred method of self-defense. He decided rather quickly to take his comfort elsewhere.

'What happened to her father?' Blunt and unexpected. Those were the questions that always brought results.

'Her . . . ' Nikki's face paled. 'Claire doesn't have a father,' she said firmly, and turned away.

'Excuse me?'

She tried to ignore him, not quite succeeding. The slight tremble in her hand as she lifted the last spoonfuls of pablum to Claire's mouth gave her away. One more push ought to do it.

'Everybody has a father, Nikki. Unless . . . '

She practically leapt out of her chair when the timer rang and hurried across the room to pull the muffins out of the oven. Saved by the bell, thought Gren, as his stomach grumbled hungrily. If they tasted even half as good as they looked and smelled . . . He smiled to himself. That was Nikki's strategy. Her way of throwing him off track. He watched in silence as she readied a bottle of milk for Claire, turned the steaming muffins out into a cloth-lined basket, and carried them to the table.

'Would you like some eggs or maybe a piece of cheese?'

'I'd like an exclusive.' *Check*.

'An ex . . . what?'

'On your story.' *And mate*.

He wouldn't have believed her already pale face had any color left to lose, but he saw the dregs drain slowly away as she sank onto the chair opposite his.

'M-my story?'

Gren reached for a muffin, breaking it open on his plate while she watched. And waited. Suddenly, this didn't feel like a winning game. But he was in too deep to quit now.

'The Immaculate Conception, Miss Larssen. It's been nearly two thousand years since the last one, y'know.'

For one long moment the kitchen fell absolutely silent. Even Claire seemed to be holding her breath. Then Nikki laughed. A measured, careful laugh that matched the very practiced blank expression she'd arranged on her face. 'Very funny.'

'Well,' said Gren, lifting a bite of rhubarb muffin to his mouth, 'you did say — mmmmm. This is good. Have some.'

'Later.' She folded her hands in her lap and drew a deep breath. 'A father doesn't abandon his own child, Mr. Wilder. A father doesn't deny knowing that child's mother. A father is a whole lot more than a wasted minute between the sheets. And anyway,' she added, her voice growing colder word-by-word, 'Claire's father is *none* of your business.'

And a very practiced story to match, thought Gren. A neat little speech. He polished off the muffin and reached for another while Nikki sat ramrod straight, still watching him.

'The courts,' he said quietly, 'have the power to make him take responsibility. And the power to make him prove his denial.'

He looked up, pondering 'wasted minutes between the sheets', the one thing she'd said that he sensed held a seed of truth. At least for her. Her cool expression was losing its edge, her bottom lip beginning to tremble. *Don't cry!* Her temper was the only thing that had kept him on his side of the table.

'We . . . we d-don't want his money. Or his name.' She pressed her palms flat against the tabletop and leaned toward him. 'That part of my life is over. I just want to forget it. Forget him. *Give me a break, okay?*'

'Nikki — '

'*No!*' Her hands clenched. She slammed both fists on the table and leaned closer, until he half-expected her to lunge at him.

'Calm down.'

'*Don't tell me what to do!*'

Gren caught her hands in his and held tight.

'You're tired. You're upset . . . and you're upsetting someone else, too.' He nodded in Claire's direction and watched as Nikki processed and reacted to his warning. She drew a deep breath and turned to look at the sprout. Claire stared back at her, wide-eyed, the half-empty bottle dangling from her mouth.

'What do you want from me?' she demanded, meeting his gaze once again, no longer fighting his hold on her.

'Want? I . . . nothing. I just thought . . . '

'*What?*'

'Nikki, it seems to me you're the one who said it helps to talk sometimes.'

She continued to stare at him, eyes blank and lifeless.

'What? Are the rules so different for you?'

When she didn't respond, he let go of her hands, rising slowly to his feet.

'Well, I'm a good listener. And I won't hurt you. Or Claire. And that's a promise you can count on.'

Stopping just long enough to fill his mug with coffee and help himself to a third muffin, Gren escaped to his study. But this time, he left the door open.

7

It's all up to you now.

Slowly, deliberately, Nikki pulled her hands away from the table and folded them in her lap. She could still feel the warm touch of Gren's fingers, his firm but gentle hands encircling her wrists with room to spare, calming, steadying, strengthening. How long had it been since she'd let someone touch her? Since anyone had bothered to try? How long since she'd really talked with another person about anything more important than the weather?

Last week she'd been so settled in her new life, it wouldn't have occurred to her to wonder. If she had, the answer wouldn't have mattered. She had Claire. And Noble, of course, with his steady, sensible advice. But now . . . Now, for the first time, she found herself wanting more. Someone to trust. Someone to . . . love?

Oh, please. Grow up! Love only happened in fairy tales, not in real life. In real life, her life anyway, you made your own happiness. And trust was earned, not given. In real life you took care of yourself — or died trying.

It's all up to you now.

She glanced over her shoulder at Claire, who stopped chewing on the wrong end of her bottle long enough to smile back. She looked so much like her mother sometimes. All long lashes and coy smiles. And, like Lainey, she knew exactly how to use them to get what she wanted. Trouble was, what Lainey wanted had got her dead.

And now Gren wanted to talk about it. Expected her to confide in him, the way he had in her. But once he knew the truth . . . Would he understand? Would he believe? Nikki let her eyes fall shut for a moment. Sometimes she found it impossible to believe herself. And now was not the time to grow careless. No more stupid mistakes. That was one promise made that she fully intended to keep.

She'd been far too willing to trust nine months ago. A stupid mistake that was nobody's fault but her own. And she'd been paying for it ever since — afraid to take another chance.

It was the right thing to do, she'd told herself back then. The smart thing. Smart and sensible. She'd packed up the baby and gone to the police.

'I think my sister's life may be in danger.'

Cool, calm, and collected. Don't give it all away. Just enough to get some help for Lainey before Frank Medici made it too late. 'She called me last night . . . she sounded so afraid. And now I can't find her.'

But the cops wanted details. And with details her story lost all credibility. After all, who worried about a sister they'd seen only once in ten years? Why was she wasting their time?

That was when she'd shown them the photo. A grainy Polaroid taken the day Lainey had made what she called her 'great escape'. She was seventeen, but looked more like twenty-five with her dark, wild, shoulder-length hair and tight leather jacket that left nothing to the imagination. It was hard to believe the skinny, redheaded kid at her side was her sister. Lainey had climbed on a bus, waved goodbye, and never once looked back. Little sister had gone home alone to face their mother. And Carl. And wait for a letter that would never come.

She hadn't seen Lainey again until last summer, on a hot afternoon in late August. An accidental meeting. Lainey had shown up at the restaurant on Cambie Street, arms loaded with bags and parcels from the best shops in old Vancouver, hugely pregnant and, Nikki thought, radiantly beautiful. Lainey didn't agree. She felt fat, ugly, and bloated, she said, and then she patted her stomach.

'Three more months. Then my little insurance policy pays off.'

'Insurance policy?'

'That's right. Never hurts to have a backup plan, right sis?'

Lainey ordered Perrier with a twist and a bowl of cold cucumber soup, dismissing the waiter with a wave. Nikki was pretty certain the gesture was meant to show off the cluster of diamonds she wore on her left hand.

'I don't understand.'

'Well, Frank wasn't entirely certain he wanted to marry an ex-exotic dancer from Calgary.'

'Ex — ' Nikki swallowed, hard. 'Exotic dancer?'

'Don't turn up your nose, Cat. It wasn't one of *those* places. This was strictly first class. All I did was dance . . . very tastefully, too. I used to make more money in one good night of tips than you make in a week of slaving over your pots and pans. *And* I met Frank. Didn't I tell you I'd find a rich man some day? One who'd take me away from all this.'

The jeweled hand gestured expansively, but Lainey's hard, bright gaze stayed fixed on Nikki, examining her scrubbed and vegetable-stained fingers, her sauce-splattered kitchen whites, her boyishly short, red hair, and finally her face.

'What the hell is that?'

She leaned across the table to poke at the fine, gold ring imbedded in Nikki's left eyebrow. 'Good grief, Cat . . . what were you thinking? Did it hurt?'

'No,' she answered, smiling faintly and giving the ring a little twist. 'It just . . . well, it seemed like a good idea at the time.'

'Yeah? Well . . . what's the point?'

'Truthfully?'

Lainey nodded, beginning to look a bit green as Nikki twisted the ring again.

'Intimidation.'

'Huh?'

'Gave me a bit of an edge at school, and even now, on the job. Sort of . . . takes people by surprise, puts them off guard. They don't know what to expect and that's good. Because then they have to deal with me. Not the package.' She looked down at herself and shrugged. It wasn't much of a package.

'The restaurant business is a man's world. Oh, sure, there are a lot more women chefs now than there used to be . . . but, in a lot of ways, it's a boys club. I learned a long time ago that you have to take your respect however you can get it.'

Lainey's mouth had fallen open as Nikki spoke. She closed it, slowly, then let a long moment pass before responding. 'We're not so different then, are we?'

Nikki smiled at her sister, at the expensive designer suit, the perfect makeup, the long, elegantly manicured nails, and that glorious, thick mane of black, curly hair, and felt about as different as it was possible to be. 'Who's Frank?'

'You'll die,' answered Lainey, then

paused while the waiter served her soup and poured sparking water into a goblet.

'You're needed in the kitchen,' he said, as a quiet aside.

Nikki scanned the room. Not exactly rush hour. 'Ask one of the guys to cover for me, okay? I need some time with my sister.'

He glanced at Lainey and nodded, his surprise as obvious as the fan of five dollar tips hanging out of his apron pocket. No surprise to Nikki. People never had believed that the two of them were really sisters.

'Frank Medici,' announced Lainey, in an exaggerated whisper. '*The* Frank Medici.'

Momentarily speechless, Nikki shot a quick glance over her shoulder. Just the mention of the name Medici made the hairs on the back of her neck prickle to attention. The most notorious crime family on the west coast, the Medici's had their nefarious fingers in a lot of legitimate pies, including some of the best restaurants in the city. She'd never suspected Winston of being the type to fall for that kind of quick fix, no matter how bad business was. But you just never knew.

'Well?' demanded Lainey, 'aren't you at least a little bit impressed?'

'I . . . impressed isn't exactly the word I'd choose. No.'

Lainey narrowed her eyes, watching Nikki intently as she leaned forward to sip her soup. 'What?' she said at last. 'You don't actually believe all that stuff in the newspapers, do you?'

'Lainey, the man's a — '

'He's a businessman. He's smart and handsome and wealthy beyond your dreams. And he treats me like I'm something special. Not like — '

Abruptly, Lainey looked away, stared out the window at the tourists on the sidewalk.

Not like Carl, thought Nikki, silently finishing the sentence. But there were other kinds of cruelty, other kinds of danger. Why hadn't Lainey learned, as she had, that the only person you could truly depend on was yourself?

'Anyway,' Lainey continued, 'he's big on family and responsibility, brought me out here from Calgary.' She stroked her stomach again. 'She's going to be beautiful, Cat. And, thanks to Frank, we won't ever have to worry about what we're going to eat for dinner, or how the rent's going to get paid. Y'know?'

She knew. This was an old pattern, and Lainey was falling right in line. 'But, Lainey, the man's a monster. They say he even — '

'Lies! All lies. They've never proven a thing!'

'Well how could they? Frank has a nasty habit of making witnesses disappear.'

Lainey slammed her spoon down and pushed away from the table. 'What's wrong with you, Cat? You're doing what you want . . . heaven knows why you want *this* . . . but can't you just be happy for me, too?'

'Calm down,' said Nikki softly,

reaching for her sister's hand.

Lainey pulled away.

'Lainey, I want to be happy for you . . . but Frank Medici scares me. And he should scare you, too.'

'He'd never hurt me.'

'Lainey . . . you're letting it happen all over again.'

'What're you talking about?'

'Just like Mom.'

'I am *nothing* like Mom,' she said, glaring angrily across the table as she stood and grabbed her purse.

'You don't have to pay — '

'Oh, yes I do!' Lainey dropped a crisp twenty dollar bill onto the table, more than twice the price of her Perrier and soup, then reached into her purse again and threw a faded photograph at Nikki. 'I told Frank I don't have any family. Guess I was right!'

Wordlessly, she collected her packages and stormed out of the restaurant, leaving Nikki to stare at the picture she would eventually show to two skeptical

Vancouver police detectives. The picture that would turn their skepticism to interest.

'Could be the one, eh?' The older of the two officers grew solemn and disappeared with the photo, leaving Nikki and his partner to stare at the scratched surface of a green metal table. Neither spoke.

She looked down at the baby, snuggled against her breast in a soft pink blanket, fast asleep. Gradually, as her mind filtered out the random clanks and shouts of the station house, the rhythmic tap-tap-tap of her companion's pen on the tabletop, and even the steady hum of the air conditioner, Nikki became aware of another sound. Not really a sound at all, more of a feeling . . . the oddest sensation. The baby stirred and suddenly she understood. It was the sound of two hearts beating — separate, but one. And the feeling was love.

'All right.' The old detective trudged wearily back into the room and sank onto a chair, shuffling some papers in a thin manilla folder before passing it to his partner.

It felt to Nikki as if he'd been gone forever. And now he was making her wait to hear what he had to say. She shifted nervously in her seat. Were they going to help her, or not?

'I, uh . . . we may have found your sister,' he said at last.

'Really? Wh — ' Looking across the table at him, she felt her moment of hope slip away. Suddenly, she knew what he was going to say, and why it was taking him so long. It was too late.

'Coroner's office picked up a woman this morning . . . floating off Wreck Beach. I'm sorry. We'll need you to make an ID.'

She stared at him, unable to speak, circling her arms protectively around Lainey's still-sleeping child, hearing her sister's voice again, as clearly as if she were there in the room with them. *It's all up to you now.*

She sat in numb silence while the two

officers took a second look at the papers in the folder, studied her for a moment, then got up and stepped into the hallway. She could hear them speaking in low, hushed tones. As if someone had died. And she shivered. That someone was Lainey.

'Frank,' said the older detective, in a voice barely louder than a whisper, 'is gonna want to talk to this one himself.'

*   *   *

Nikki didn't look up when Gren entered the room. If he had to guess, he'd say she hadn't moved at all in the half hour since he'd left her, except to fold her hands in her lap. They were clenched in a tight, angry knot. Head bowed, her short dark hair fell forward across her face, hiding her eyes. He wondered if she might finally have fallen asleep.

He looked at the sprout, flaked out in her highchair, one arm curled beneath her head, chewing lazily on the wrong end of her bottle. She gave him a sleepy smile and bounced to attention.

'Shhhh.' Gren raised one finger to his lips, silently crossing the room to pick up. He half-expected her to make a fuss, wail for her mother, and land him in trouble again. Instead, Claire reached out to him, curled her tiny arms around his neck, and rested her head on his shoulder. She breathed a soft, contented little sigh.

It was the sigh that did it, he decided later. Like the brush of an angel's wing against his cheek, awakening all the old memories, every tender and protective fatherly feeling he'd ever had. 'Shhhh,' he repeated, 'Mommy's sleeping. Let's take a walk, okay?'

He paused, about to bump the screen door open with his toe. Bad idea. Its patented squeak was a guaranteed sleep disturber. He retraced his steps across the kitchen, headed down the hall, past his office, through the bedroom and out the sliding glass doors. Becca's rose garden was in full bloom, the air heavy with perfume, a scent that always reminded him of her. Over the years, he'd grown to hate roses — beauty hiding thorns to prick his conscience. But things were different now. He drew a deep breath and let himself remember the good times they'd shared.

Claire began to squirm. 'Ga-ga,' she said firmly, patting his cheeks and bouncing in his arms, clearly impatient for the promised walk.

'Okay, Sprout, let's go.'

Claire shrieked with delight as he swung her up onto his shoulders. She grabbed two fists full of hair and practically wrapped herself around his head, giggling nonstop.

What was it about a child's laughter, wondered Gren, making his fifth lap around the Norway maple, that could entice a grown man to go galloping around a tree in broad daylight, making horsy noises? Damned if he knew . . . and damned if he wasn't winded.

Gently lifting Claire off his shoulders, he sank onto the grass, leaning back against the broad trunk of the old maple. It took a couple of tries and one almost-profanity to coax her tiny fingers out of his hair — until she saw the dandelions nodding in the grass. A moment later, she was perched contentedly on his knee, studying yellow petals with rapt attention and slightly crossed eyes.

Watching her, Gren's thoughts wandered — not to his own daughter, although Amy was never far from his mind when the sprout was around — but to Claire's father. Did he know what he was missing? Did he care? What had made Nikki run from him? What kept her in hiding? And then, surprisingly, he found himself considering the possibility that it wasn't the man she was afraid of at all. That maybe she was afraid of getting caught.

Wasn't it possible, just possible, that she'd stolen the child? It happened all the time — a marriage on the rocks, the threat of a custody battle . . . Maybe

Nikki had lost that battle, taken matters into her own hands. He brushed a wisp of hair off the sprout's face, picked her another dandelion, and let himself wonder where her father was right now, if he was thinking about her. And grieving.

It wouldn't be hard to check a few databases for missing and abducted children. And he still had contacts at the newspaper who'd be willing to help without asking too many questions. He brushed Claire's cheek again, not entirely certain he wanted to open this particular can of worms. Because as strongly as every instinct warned him that Nikki was hiding something, another, stronger, certainty had begun to grow in the short time he'd known her. She was a good and decent person.

'*Claire?!*'

Nikki's panic-stricken shriek brought Gren to his feet already running, with Claire tucked under his arm like a football. A giggling, wriggling football. They made it halfway across the wide expanse of lawn before the screen door slammed.

Gren looked up and froze in his tracks. Bearing down on him, fists clenched and green eyes blazing, was the super-mom herself. Even at this distance, he could see her nostrils flaring. Thank goodness she wasn't packing iron. He had to say something. *Anything*. Head her off at the pass! Better still, hide behind the baby. He did, and tried to smile.

'*What are you doing?*'

'I — '

'Don't you ever — *ever* — touch her again! Do you hear me?'

Nikki snatched the child from his arms as she spoke — or tried to. Claire latched onto the front of his shirt and howled.

'We were just — '

'*Let go of her!*'

'I'm not — ' No. Now was not the time to point out the obvious. Prying tiny fingers loose, he passed the sprout to Nikki.

'Calm down,' he said softly. 'We were just getting some air while you were asleep.'

Claire wailed, reaching out to him, red-faced and sobbing, her cheeks flecked with bits of dandelion petal and streaked with tears. He wouldn't be able to resist her much longer. Or her mother either. The urge to comfort them was almost overwhelming.

'I was n-not s-sleeping,' said Nikki, folding the screaming child in her arms and backing slowly away. 'I j-just . . . I — '

In the split second before her knees buckled under her, Nikki's pale face wore an expression of utter horror.

8

'Nikki?'

'I'm f-fine.' *Liar*.

'You are not fine. You're . . . exhausted. And scared half to death. And . . . '

Gren tightened his hold on her. She heard him make a little groan, barely audible, before he continued. 'And it's my fault. Stupid thing to do. Sorry.'

'*Let go!*' Good grief, one little lapse, one rubber-kneed moment of after-shock, and the man acted as if he expected her to fall apart. Or fall over. She tried to shrug him off and wobbled again. *Damn!* 'I'm fine.'

'Okay.'

'*Really*.'

'I know.'

'Don't patronize me.'

'I'm not patronizing, I'm . . . '

'What? You're *what?*'

'Apologizing.'

161

Oh, boy. He sounded like he meant it, too.

He didn't let go of her until they reached the back porch steps and, even then, one hand hovered close to Claire's shoulder. Just in case, she supposed. Well, at least the man had his priorities straight.

She glanced up at him as she sank onto the top step and saw his gaze flicker quickly away. Shoving his hands into his pockets, he pretended to study the sky, but she could feel him watching again as she pulled the tail of her T-shirt out of her jeans and used it to dry Claire's face. The baby had stopped crying at last, settling on a wide-eyed, determined pout. Nikki sighed. Barely nine months old and already a master of the fine art of button pushing.

'Look, I — ' Her explanation collided head-on with his.

'It's just — Sorry,' muttered Gren. 'You first.' He sat on the step beside her, resting his elbows on his knees and staring off into the distance.

Just . . . what? wondered Nikki. Why was this so hard? The man had stolen Claire and disappeared without a word. On the other hand, there was no denying that she'd overreacted to the whole situation. By a country mile. Or two.

'Okay, maybe . . . maybe I am tired. A little,' she admitted, hoping the silent battle she was waging with Claire wasn't as obvious from Gren's vantage point. From the moment he'd joined them on the steps, the child had been determined to escape onto his lap. And Nikki was just as determined to prevent that from happening. Maybe he wouldn't look. Wrong.

He glanced sideways and smiled, made an involuntary, almost instinctive, gesture of welcome, then abruptly withdrew. Claire whimpered and squirmed, all seventeen pounds of her focused on her goal, just inches out of reach — a friendly, male knee, wearing threadbare blue jeans. The owner of the knee sighed loudly.

'Oh, for heaven's sake, Gren. I didn't really mean you couldn't touch her. I was . . . I just . . . oh, here!'

The battle lost, she lifted Claire onto his knee and watched the two of them grin at each other like a couple of Cheshire Cats. Too irritating for words. Attachments weren't part of the plan. Neither was the warm and fuzzy, comfortable feeling she had every time she saw them together. What the heck was that, anyway?

Nikki tried, but couldn't look away. How would it feel to be part of the magic they seemed to share? To have Gren Wilder look at *her*, eyes full of love and longing, to feel the gentle touch of his hands, his lips, to lose herself in his embrace . . .

She squared her shoulders, drew a deep breath, and forced herself to stop wondering. Those were things that could never be, for his sake as much as for hers. But she did still owe him an apology.

'I shouldn't have said what I did,

okay? But you shouldn't have taken her like that.'

'I — '

'*Don't interrupt.*'

He lifted one eyebrow and cracked a half-smile. 'Yes ma'am.'

Nikki ignored the sarcasm in favor of his lopsided grin. Hadn't she said all along that she'd learn to hate that grin? It made her feel uncomfortable. Not to mention uncomfortably warm. *No!* She wasn't about to travel that road again.

'As I was saying . . . I just needed a minute or two. To unwind. Claire was perfectly happy and safe in her highchair. I'd have heard her if she needed me, y'know. It was just . . . it was our quiet time. And then you . . . I turned around and she was . . . she was gone. *Gone.* Do you know what that felt like?'

His grin vanished, swept away in a rush of emotion so painful she could almost feel it. She watched him struggle for control, watched his jaw clench and his mouth tighten in a pale, thin line.

The light in his warm, brown eyes flickered and died. And it was all her fault.

'Oh, Gren. I'm so sorry. I didn't mean . . . '

'It's okay. You're right. I wasn't thinking. Like I said, stupid mistake.'

He forced a smile and stood up, depositing Claire on Nikki's lap. 'Won't happen again. I'd better get back to work.'

His eyes, heavy with sorrow, made a lie of the smile.

'I'm sorry, pumpkin,' whispered Nikki, as the door slammed shut behind him. 'I'm sorry I yelled . . . sorry I frightened you.' She watched through the screen until Gren disappeared down the hall to his office, then said it again. For him this time. 'I'm sorry . . . '

Claire seemed unimpressed, but didn't complain when Nikki pulled her close for a hug. They were going to have to be more careful from now on, that was all. Get back into their normal, pre-Gren routine. Happy and busy.

Too busy to fall in love with the monumentally confusing new man in their lives. It wouldn't be fair to let the attachment grow. Tempting, maybe, but not fair. It would hurt too much when the time came to leave. And Gren Wilder had already had more than enough hurt in his life.

Leaning back against the railing, she hugged Claire a little tighter and said a quiet thank you to the man. He'd just given her the worst scare she'd had in months, but he'd also opened her eyes to the grim reality of their situation. It could've been worse. *Much* worse.

★ ★ ★

'Frank,' said the older detective, in a voice barely louder than a whisper, 'is gonna want to talk to this one himself.'

Nikki never could remember exactly how she'd managed to get out of her chair and across the room. Those moments were gone forever, lost somewhere in the chaos of her own dreadful imaginings of the scene at Wreck Beach. Dark water and Lainey's cold body. Black hair floating lifeless on the waves, like limp seaweed. But she would never forget the look of shocked surprise on the detectives' faces when she suddenly appeared in the doorway.

'I'm sorry,' she said in a quiet, hesitant voice, 'but I need some time alone before . . . before we go to the m-morgue.' She took a minute to steady her breathing. Would they buy it? Believe the grief-stricken sister? 'My, um . . . my baby. She needs to nurse . . . '

'No problem,' said the pencil tapper. 'Use the interview room. Close the door.'

Her bottom lip trembled, hot tears welled up in her eyes as the last shreds of self-control slipped away. *Use it!* Blinking, she let the tears trickle slowly down her cheeks. 'N-no. I need to change her. And wash up. Is there a lady's room?'

The two cops exchanged glances,

then studied her for an unbearably long moment before the senior detective pointed to their left. 'Sure. Around the corner. We'll wait.'

She turned and walked away, forcing herself to take one slow step at a time until she'd turned the corner. Just as she remembered, the washroom was right next to the stairwell. She gave the door a shove as she passed, then bolted down the steps, glad, for once, of her sensible and very quiet rubber-soled kitchen shoes. If one of the cops had followed to keep an eye on her, he'd see the washroom door drifting shut and figure she'd gone in.

What would she do if the baby started to cry? Would her arms and the soft pink blanket be enough to muffle the sound? She ran, praying she wouldn't have to find out, and kept running until she reached the first floor lobby. The stairwell was quiet and, by some miracle, little Cat was quiet, too. Wide awake, but quiet. Too frightened to cry?

Nikki pushed the door open. The room beyond was crowded with people, lined up at the information desk or just waiting their turn at the coffee concession. From where she stood, every last one of them looked remarkably like Frank Medici.

Fifteen minutes later, still breathless from a panicked run through the back alleys of Gastown, Nikki was formulating the beginnings of a plan. A plan that would take her down a very different path from the one she'd intended to travel. In a perfect world, she'd still be on the road to Paris — Le Cordon Bleu — a hard-won dream come true. But now . . . she would simply disappear.

She glanced down at the child in her arms, all alone in the world, except for her. Why was it that, suddenly, nothing else seemed to matter?

They were safe, for the moment at least, in the hot and bustling kitchen of Winston's Cambie Street restaurant. Nikki sat with her back to the wall, keeping watch on the door as the baby sucked hungrily on a bottle.

She thought about Lainey, about that last phone call. She thought about the gym bag, stashed in her locker not six feet away, hiding her sister's latest, and last, 'insurance policy'. *'See for yourself,'* Lainey had said. *'It's under the blankets in little Cat's travel bed. It's all up to you now.'*

Poor Lainey had been so certain it would keep them safe. Nikki was just as certain it would only get them killed. She almost wished she'd left it at the apartment for Frank to find. But it was too late for that. She wouldn't risk going back. Not now. Not ever.

'Just tell me one thing,' said Garth the sous chef, wiping his hands on a towel as he sat down beside her. 'How am I supposed to help you out if I don't even know what's going on?'

Garth was a bearded, barrel-chested man, who wore his shoulder-length greying hair in a ponytail, and flaunted the jailhouse tattoo on his hand like a personal badge of honor. He stared at the child in Nikki's arms with obvious fascination, as if he'd never seen a baby before. 'Well?'

'Only what you need to know,' said Nikki, glancing pointedly at the back of his hand before meeting his gaze. 'I never once asked you.'

He studied her for one long moment, then smiled. 'Fair enough. So? What d'you need?'

'I need to stop being me. So that means new ID . . . for myself and the baby.'

He nodded. 'Do-able. What else?'

She gulped a quick breath. Do-able. Just like that. It wasn't supposed to be this easy, was it? 'And I need to get out of the city. Fast. Without being seen.'

'No problem. What else?'

'What else?' Garth made her impossibilities seem like everyday requests. 'I — ' She shrugged. It wasn't that much of a plan yet. 'I don't know.'

'Well, for starters, lose the eyebrow ring. It's too, uh . . . memorable. And while you're at it,' he added quietly, reaching over to tousle her hair, 'you'd better do something about the carrot top.'

*   *   *

'Lookin' a might peaked today, Missy. But you just have yourself one of these. That'll fix what ails ya.'

Peaked? Talk about understatement. She'd nearly jumped out of her skin a moment ago, when Noble's hand had brushed her hair.

'Nothing 'ails' me, Noble. I'm perfectly fine. Just a little tired, that's all.'

Nikki peeked into the basket he'd set on the top step and smiled. 'Mmmmm, tomatoes. They look wonderful. Boy! They even smell wonderful. From your garden?'

'Yep.' He grinned. 'Wait'll you taste 'em. Mouth full of sunshine, Missy.' Winking, he reached for Claire and lifted her into his arms. 'You're more'n just tired, though, if y'ask me. Which, a'course, you didn't.'

She should have seen that one coming. Noble was obviously on another fishing expedition. Sighing, Nikki pushed wearily to her feet. 'Stay for tea?'

'Yep.' Balancing Claire on his shoulder, Noble followed her into the kitchen and parked himself at the end of the pine table. 'Been workin' too hard then?'

'I suppose. All those special orders for the party at Ravensleigh kind of messed up my schedule.'

'And then there's Gren, a'course.'

Nikki shot him a dark glance. 'We hardly know he's here, most of the time.' Huh! If she was going to lie, she'd better sound a little more convincing.

'So he tells me,' said Noble, waggling his eyebrows.

'He — What are you talking about? When did you speak to Gren?'

'Well, just now Missy. What, he didn't tell you he was goin' down to Toronto?'

'He is?'

'Already gone.'

In spite of herself, Nikki's gaze traveled to the open door at the end of the kitchen. 'He didn't . . . I mean . . . well, he . . . he doesn't have to tell me every time he goes out. Unless . . . you know, he doesn't want a meal . . . or something.' *Get a grip!* She squared her shoulders. 'Where Mr. Wilder goes is his business. Not mine. I'm sure it never even occurred to him to tell me. And it certainly wouldn't occur to me to ask.'

She poured boiling water over tea bags in an old Brown Betty pot and carried it to the table. What on earth was the matter with her? The man had left without saying a word. Well, so what? It was his house, his life. Why on earth should she care? Looking up, she found Noble studying her, wearing an understanding and particularly annoying expression.

'Well,' he said thoughtfully, 'that's why I'm here, don't y'know.'

'*What?*' Surely Gren hadn't called on

Noble to babysit while he was gone. 'I'm perfectly fine. And perfectly able to take care of myself. And Claire. *Honestly*. The man makes me so . . . so . . . '

'Able? Well, a'course y'are, Missy. Nobody ever said you weren't.' Noble's expression grew puzzled. 'I been takin' care of that old car of his, is all. He phones just a bit ago, asks me to bring it on over. And then our Gren says he's got some work to take care of, research or something. Has to go down to the paper, use one of them 'data bases'. Then he offers to drive me home.' Noble shrugged, pausing a moment to watch Claire as she snapped his suspenders. His exaggerated 'Ouch!' had her giggling and trying again.

'No, says I, I'm fixin' to visit with Nikki and Claire. So Gren, he says to me, 'Good. Nikki's been working too hard.' An' that's all. What's got the bee in your bonnet?'

'I don't — '

Noble stopped bouncing Claire and

narrowed his eyes. 'Had a bit of a spat, then, did ya?'

'Spat? All right. What did he say to you?'

'Oh, for pity sake. The boy said nothin' I can't see with my own two eyes.' He chuckled. 'Suppose the two of you'll see it, too. Eventually.'

'See it?' She caught the twinkle in his eye just in time to bite back the rest of her sarcastic response. It was plain to see where Claire was learning her button pushing finesse. Turning, Nikki stomped across the room to get mugs and milk for their tea and a bottle of juice for the baby.

'Why don't we just drop that subject,' she said firmly, ignoring the chuckle that followed her across the kitchen.

'Oh fine, fine . . . suspect it must be hard for you now, though, knowin' the truth and all.'

Oh, boy. Seemed as if there was just no avoiding it. She handed the juice to Claire and poured their tea, then sank onto her chair. 'What truth is that,

Noble?' As if she didn't know.

'I ask, he tells me it's all out in the open now. Y'know . . . all about his Becca and their sweet Amy. Then I see the way he looks at you and the little one b'fore he drives away. And I'm thinkin', that's just what the two of you need.'

The way he looked at us? *No! Don't go there.*

'In case you haven't noticed, Noble Bateman, I *don't* need a man to take care of me. I can — '

'Take care of yourself. Yes. I know. I've seen you do it.' He smiled down at Claire and slowly shook his head. 'But, Missy, you both need someone to love.'

9

Steak and mushroom pie. Nikki ran her thumb across the neatly printed label, smoothing down the edges as she added the plastic-wrapped dish to the stack in the freezer. Last one. *Minute Meals* were ready for the next two weeks. Not bad for three days work.

She tugged at the blue paisley kerchief tied around her head, pulling it off and shoving it into her pocket. Ugly thing. And uncomfortable, too. But better then risking a strand of black hair in the food. Black with red roots, that is. It was way past time to take care of that little problem, but first . . .

Sighing, she sank onto a chair at the table and ran her fingers through her hair, stopping to rest with her head in her hands. First came the daunting task of cleaning up the kitchen, a mess that could only be described as post apocalyptic.

Thank goodness Gren was still away. Life was so much simpler without him. Her gaze drifted, unbidden, to the door at the end of the room. *Much simpler*. No one to care if the house was a mess or if the cleanup got left for tomorrow. Not that he was likely to care. No one to complain if breakfast was late or if dinner didn't turn out quite right. Not that he'd ever once complained. Nobody watching, nobody listening . . . nobody.

She glanced at Claire, who was absently brushing flour off the tabletop, watching it drift like powdered snow onto the terra cotta floor. The baby had been strangely quiet for the last couple of days. Moody and endlessly cranky. And Raggedy Man, never far out of reach, was now stuck like glue on glue, a permanent fixture in the crook of her left arm.

So much for getting back to the way things used to be. The busy part was no problem, but 'happy' was beginning to feel like an insurmountable challenge.

Why was she letting this happen? Good grief, in their few short days together, Gren Wilder had managed to turn their lives upside-down. And then what did he do? He ran away. Typical man.

Oh, he'd called that first night. And with a perfectly reasonable explanation. His work at the paper was taking longer than he'd expected. So, instead of commuting from Vinegar Hill, he'd be staying in the city with Aprile. Perfectly reasonable. After all, he hadn't seen his sister for nearly six years. They'd have a lot of catching up to do. And there was certainly nothing to hold him at Wilder House. Nothing at all.

Nikki leapt to her feet and grabbed the broom, churning up little tornados of flour as she swept. Was it possible that she was actually missing the man? *No way!* He was endlessly annoying, always butting in, always watching. And then there was that crooked little grin . . .

She swept a bit faster. Anyway, they barely knew each other. And, with the possible exception of his gentle way with Claire, she had no reason to think he'd turn out to be any different than all the rest. More trouble than he was worth. Just one more mess to sweep out of her life.

Behind her, something hit the floor with a metallic clatter. Claire must have finished 'cleaning up' the pastry mat and moved on to the utensils. Nikki turned just in time to see the baby sneeze. Claire looked momentarily surprised and then rubbed both eyes with her fists.

Well, darn. No wonder the poor kid was sneezing. The air was hazy with flour, thanks to her frenzy of sweeping. She propped the broom against the table and scooped Claire out of the highchair. 'I don't know about you, pumpkin, but I think we deserve a break.'

Claire sneezed again.

'Yup,' said Nikki, grabbing the paisley kerchief to wipe the baby's nose, 'something to take our minds off . . . Well, whatever. Let's go for a drive. I think it's time you discovered chocolate ice cream.'

Minutes later they were on the road, Claire contentedly watching the trees pass by her window, and Nikki waging a hopeless battle to coax a little speed out of her old blue van. It had taken three tries to get it started and the muffler sounded as if it might actually fall off this trip. It sure wasn't much of a getaway vehicle. Not much of a delivery van for *Minute Meals*, either. She was going to have to put some money into repairs, and soon.

Lost in thoughts of mufflers and reliable transportation, Nikki didn't notice the aging red Mustang as it approached on the opposite side of the road. But its lone occupant noticed her. He slowed the car to a crawl as they passed and paused to watch in his rearview mirror as the blue van stalled at the stop sign, then lurched around the corner on the road to Vinegar Hill.

★ ★ ★

'What the — ' For the second time in less than two weeks, Nikki felt her heart thud to a fleeting but painful halt. She slammed her foot down on the brake and swore as the van immediately stalled again. Claire giggled, waving a pink plastic spoon in the air and thumping both feet against the front of her car seat.

'Shhhhhh,' whispered Nikki, as her heart and her brain shuddered back into gear. She stared at the red car, parked in her usual spot near the kitchen door. She'd never seen it around town before. Most of the old-timers drove pick-up trucks or station wagons, like Noble did. And the new people, the *Minute Meals* people, had more expensive taste. No, this was a stranger. And strangers meant . . . oh, no! What if one of Frank's thugs had finally found them?

For the first time since their arrival in Vinegar Hill, she wished that Wilder

House wasn't so thoroughly hidden from view. If only she could've seen that car from the road and kept right on driving. Instead, they were trapped. Prisoners on a narrow gravel laneway. A couple of ducks lined up in a neat little row.

The baby thumped her feet again, impatient. 'Right,' whispered Nikki, 'do something.' *But what?*

She'd never been any good at backing up, even worse in this old monster of a van. She'd probably land them in the ditch and, after all the rain last weekend, they wouldn't get out again without a winch.

She glanced at Claire, who was happily sucking on the pink spoon, chin still coated with the evidence of her first encounter with chocolate. Unbuckling her seatbelt, Nikki slipped into the back of the van to lock the doors, then reached across Claire to crank up the window.

'Hang on,' she said, and bit down on her lip as she jiggled the key in the

185

ignition. The engine sputtered and died.

'No! Not now!' She tried again and the unmistakable smell of gasoline filled the air. The stupid engine was flooded. Count to ten. Pedal to the floor. Turn the key and keep cranking. She held her breath, painfully aware of each second ticking away. All she had to do was get to the yard, then she could turn the van around and make a run for it. Trouble was, whoever belonged to that red car had probably already heard the clatter.

The engine turned over. She gulped a deep breath, shoved the stick shift into first, and hit the gas. It was just too bad they'd have to leave Lainey's 'insurance' behind, because it was a sure bet that Frank Medici and his pals wouldn't be smart enough to find it on their own.

She popped the clutch. The tires bit into the gravel as the old van lurched, hesitated, then tore into the yard. *Too fast!*

Hand-over-hand she cranked the

wheel, every ounce of her strength focused on steering the van in a tight arc across the yard — half a ton of metal that had suddenly sprouted wings. But she wouldn't risk another stall. Not here. Not now. She forced her foot away from the brake.

The van's rusty, dented bumper whizzed past the polished rear end of the red Mustang, missing it by a whisker, sending a hail of gravel onto the lawn, the flower beds, even as far as the back porch. They weren't going to make it.

As that thought, and all the frightening consequences that went along with it, took shape in her mind, Nikki felt the van begin to shudder. It slid sideways, skittering across the yard like a stone over water. Another second and they'd be on the lawn, aiming straight for that old Norway maple. Or worse, diving headlong into the pond. She hit the brakes with both feet.

After the engine died, the van made one last half-turn in clumsy slow motion. The crunch of gravel gave way to a deafening silence. Through the lingering dust cloud, Nikki saw a shadowy figure lurking beyond the kitchen door. Desperate for a way out, her gaze flew from the doorway to the Mustang. She stared for a seemingly endless moment at the blue and white Ontario plate on the back bumper and felt a groan rise in her throat. This couldn't be happening. She rubbed her eyes and looked again, suddenly wanting a lot more than just escape. She wanted to sink right through the floor of the van and disappear. Forever.

The Mustang wore a vanity plate. And it said 'Wilder'.

*　*　*

Nikki wasn't certain how long she'd been sitting there, her hands still clenched, white-knuckled, around the steering wheel. Probably not more than a few minutes. But it felt like a lifetime. She'd done it again, let her fear and paranoia get the best of her, jumped to all the wrong conclusions . . . Why was it so impossible to believe they were really safe here? And how was she ever going to explain this to Gren?

He already suspected her of hiding something, and strange behavior was the quickest way to convince him he was right. She tried to imagine her near collision with the Mustang, complete with squealing brakes and clouds of dust, from his point of view. Couldn't get much stranger, she decided.

Sighing, she peeled her fingers off the wheel and looked over at Claire. The baby grinned back at her, bouncing and waving both hands in the air — Claire talk for 'do it again!' Apparently their little game of spin the truck was the most fun she'd had in days.

'You've got to be kidding,' grumbled Nikki as she pulled the baby out of her car seat. 'That was definitely a once in a lifetime ride, kiddo. At least, I sure hope it was.'

She pushed the door open and slid

out of the van, balancing Claire on her hip. No sign of Gren's shadow beyond the screen, but she was certain he was still there. Watching. She could feel him. By the time she reached the back porch her face was hot with embarrassment.

She sighed, making a half-hearted swipe at Claire's chocolate-covered chin, wishing she'd thought to bring along a wash cloth. Seemed it wasn't enough she'd acted like a fool, now they'd have to look the part, too. Catching the corner of the screen door with her toe, she nudged it open and stepped inside. Mercifully — miraculously — the kitchen was empty.

Gren watched from the shadows of the dining room as Nikki crossed the kitchen to the sink. She sat Claire down on the counter and twisted the tap, glancing over her shoulder a couple of times at the doorway to his rooms as she waited for the water to warm up. Never once did she think to check in the other direction.

Now what? If he said something, he'd only frighten her. Again. And judging from her panicked reaction to the car parked at the back door, she'd had more than her share of fright for one night. Who or what was she so afraid of? After three days of painful research, he was no closer to the truth.

He'd learned more than he ever wanted to know about missing children, about desperate parents, faint hope, and grim statistics. Most of those missing kids would never be seen again. But in the end he was convinced that Claire was not one of them. Whatever Nikki was hiding, or hiding from, was still a mystery. A mystery he was more determined than ever to unravel. Without frightening her.

He stayed quiet until he imagined her turning around, imagined her reaction when she saw him and realized he'd been watching. Not a pleasant thought. Gren cleared his throat and saw her shoulders stiffen.

'You're back,' she said quietly, using

the corner of a towel to mop something brown and obviously sticky off the baby's face.

'Yes. And so are you.' He bit back a laugh. 'Quite an entrance. I didn't know you were into that kind of thing.'

She didn't turn around. 'What kind of thing?'

'Demolition derby.'

She stopped mopping.

'Gotta tell you, you had me worried there for a minute. Thought the old Mustang was a goner.'

'I . . . Sorry. I was a little worried myself. For a minute.'

He stepped out of the shadows and crossed the kitchen to stand close behind her. She took a deep breath — two deep breaths — before hoisting Claire onto her hip and turning to face him. He tried not to stare at the brown smudge on her chin.

'It was the, um, uh . . . the clutch, I think. Stupid truck stalled, and then . . . and then . . . What's so funny?'

In an instant her expression changed

from embarrassed to annoyed. Gren knew he was fighting a losing battle. The smirk he'd been wearing erupted into a hearty laugh, while Claire, still sticky, tried her darndest to launch herself out of Nikki's arms and into his.

'Oh, no you don't! Not until your Mom gets you cleaned up. What've you two been into, Sprout?'

Claire squealed and tried again.

'Ice cream,' said Nikki, looking more than a little peeved. 'Chocolate. I think she liked it. Hold still, darn it!'

'Here, let me.' Taking the wet towel from Nikki's hand, Gren finished wiping Claire's chin, then lifted the baby into his arms. 'All done. What about you?'

'What? What about me?'

He was battling the laugh again, barely able to look her in the eye. 'Did you like it, too?' His gaze drifted to the chocolaty dribble on her chin.

'I . . . aw . . .'

Uh-oh, thought Gren. The light dawns. He flipped the towel over, found a fresh corner to wipe the chocolate away. To his surprise Nikki just stood there, red-faced and speechless, while Claire giggled. Time to change the subject.

'So, um . . . what happened here?' He gestured around the kitchen. 'Some sort of freak baking accident? Cake blew up on you or . . . '

She pursed her lips as if about to tell him off, then gave a helpless little shrug instead. 'Two weeks worth of *Minute Meals* happened, that's what. I figured the cleanup could wait until all the work was done.'

'Oh. And is it?'

'Is it what?'

'Done. The work, I mean.'

She nodded, planting both hands on her hips. Gren took a step back and pretended to concentrate on playing with the sprout. He wondered if Nikki realized how angry that stance made her look, and quickly decided that she probably did.

'We needed a break. If I'd known you

were coming home, I'd have cleaned up the mess before we went. You didn't call.'

'I don't really care. About the mess, I mean. But — '

'But what?' she snapped, before he could finish his sentence.

'D'you think things might be back to normal by tomorrow night?'

'I suppose so. Why?'

This, thought Gren, was where things got interesting. He was about to discover just how far Miss Nikki Larssen was willing to carry the role of chief cook and bottle washer. 'I'm expecting a guest for dinner.'

'Oh? Is Mrs. Massey — '

'No. Not Aprile. This is someone . . . special. And I'd like to make a good impression.'

★   ★   ★

'I'll give him good impression,' grumbled Nikki, cramming the scrub brush and bucket into the broom closet and flopping onto a chair. It was past midnight, but she'd finally finished the mammoth cleanup and, more importantly, Claire was finally asleep. It would be a good long time before that child saw chocolate ice cream again. The sugar buzz had lasted hours beyond her usual bedtime.

Resting her chin in her hands, Nikki studied the menu for tomorrow's 'special' dinner, scribbled on a decidedly unspecial scrap of brown grocery bag. Salmon Florentine en croute with scalloped potatoes. Salad and grilled tomatoes, fresh from Noble's garden, of course. And sour cherry tarts for dessert. She'd have to make a quick trip to town for a nice bottle of wine . . . or maybe Gren would want to do that himself. A personal choice for his special someone.

She made a face. It was all so sappy. The way he'd fussed over every detail, rejected one suggestion after another until they'd finally settled on the salmon. And then he'd had the nerve to ask if she'd mind wearing a dress. *You do have a dress, don't you Nikki?* Honestly!

Just who was this special person, anyway? Someone from his past? A new conquest? She'd probably be tall. And drop dead gorgeous, with perfect cheekbones and long, wavy hair, and . . . Nikki looked down at her nearly flat chest and sighed. And a figure. With luck, she might even have a brain.

'Nice,' she muttered, pushing away from the table. 'Care to try meowing, now?' What did it matter who he brought home? Or when? Or why? She didn't care . . . or shouldn't. This was only a job. The man was her boss. And that strange little bite in the pit of her stomach was certainly not jealousy. Only indigestion. Nothing more. This date of his was the best thing that could have happened. And not a minute too soon. It was bad enough that Claire was smitten with the man. She had no intention of getting all puppy-eyed over him, too.

Nikki left the scribbled menu on the table and turned out the kitchen light. It was about time she started remembering all the promises she'd made to herself. Noble was wrong. She didn't need, or want, a man in her life. And as for Gren Wilder and his special someone . . . well, he'd have his good impression. Little black dress and all.

10

'Wine? Uh . . . '

He looked as if he'd never heard the word before.

Nikki finished smoothing the soft linen cloth across the dining room table and stood back to watch as Gren smoothed it again. And again. If the man didn't stop 'helping', and soon, she wouldn't have a lip left to chew on.

Satisfied at last, he opened the silverware drawer and turned to stare blankly at the contents, ignoring Claire's impatient tugging on the cuff of his jeans.

'Yes, Gren. Wine. You know . . . fruit of the vine, juice of the grape — '

He flashed her a warning glance. '*What kind?*'

Now they were getting somewhere. She thought for a moment.

'Something crisp, not too sweet

. . . maybe a Chardonnay.'

'Chardonnay. But that's . . . white.'

Make that getting nowhere. 'Well, you are having fish . . . '

'I like red.'

'Okay.' What had she ever done to deserve this? 'Get red then.'

'With fish?'

Good grief! It wasn't even noon yet. Was he going to keep this up for another eight hours? The dull headache she'd been fighting all morning began to throb.

He turned to look at her, both hands full of cutlery. Nikki took a deep breath and tried to smile. 'White is suggested, but it's not carved in stone. You should have what you like. Salad fork on the outside.'

'But what if she doesn't like it? Uh . . . what fork?'

Nikki flopped onto the closest chair and hauled Claire up onto her lap. Maybe he'd like to make the salmon himself, too. Then she could just take the afternoon off. 'I thought you said this was somebody special. Salad fork . . . the small one.'

Gren dumped the silverware in a heap on the table and frowned at her. 'What, you can't be special if you don't like white wine?'

'That's not what I meant. You have met this person before, right? So . . . Don't you know what she likes?'

He didn't answer, just looked doubtful, confused. Surely this wasn't their first date, or worse — 'This isn't some kind of fix-up is it? A blind date?'

'No! It's just . . . it never came up. This one?' He held up a dessert fork.

'No.' She pressed the palm of her hand against her temple, tried not to groan as the pain behind her eyes spiked again. 'Just let me set the table, okay? And why don't you get both.'

'Both?'

'Sure. Buy a bottle of your favorite red, and get a nice Chardonnay, too. That way she can have whatever she likes.'

He dropped the fork and shoved his

hands into his pockets. 'You're upset.'

Yes! 'I am not — *Hey!*' She caught Claire's hands just in time. Another second and Gren's neatly smoothed table cloth would have hit the floor, dessert forks and all. He looked slightly panicked at the prospect.

'I'm not upset,' she finished, folding her arms around the squirming baby. 'Why would I be?'

'I'm in your way.'

You've got that right. Her chewed lip was beginning to hurt almost as much as her head.

'You think I'm being foolish.'

Right again. 'I think you're nervous. And, honestly, I don't understand why.'

He looked puzzled.

'I mean, you must like her . . . right? Or you wouldn't have invited her to dinner.'

'Well . . . yeah.'

'And if she didn't like you, she wouldn't have accepted.'

'Well, she . . . ' He swallowed, hard. 'I guess.'

More than puzzled, the man looked petrified. Suddenly she felt almost sorry for him. Maybe it was a first date. The first since his wife died. And that had to be difficult, no matter how well he knew the special someone.

'Dinner will be perfect,' she said softly. 'I promise. And don't worry about Claire. She'll forget all about the table cloth in a minute or two. Why don't you go get that wine? And try to relax, okay?'

'Okay.' His forced smile wasn't even halfway crooked. 'Maybe the sprout could come with me?' He sounded hopeful, brushed Claire's cheek with his fingers as he met Nikki's gaze.

'I don't think so.' Why was he doing this now?

'She could keep me company . . . it'd get both of us out of your way.'

'She's not in my way. And she's not your responsibility. She's mine.' Why had she said that? It sounded so defensive. A simple 'no' would have been enough.

Gren's jaw tightened. He took a step back, his gaze still locked on hers. 'I'm only trying to help. I enjoy spending time with her. And, in case you haven't noticed, she likes me.'

Of course she likes you, thought Nikki, growing more uncomfortable by the second. What's not to like? *No way!* She hadn't just thought that, hadn't almost said it out loud. It had to be the headache. Suddenly the room seemed very small, she felt trapped, pressured, confused. What was he staring at? What was he reading on her face, in her eyes?

She looked away, relieved to break even that small contact, and rose slowly to her feet. 'It's almost time for her lunch, anyway.' She cleared her throat, hating the nervous edge that had crept into her voice, hating the resigned sigh he made as she brushed past on her way to the kitchen. 'And if you want her quiet when your company comes tonight, we'd better just stick to routine.'

This might be the stupidest thing he'd ever done. Gren stared at his reflection in the mirror. A pair of dark, deer-in-the-headlights eyes stared back at him from a freshly-shaved face. No 'might be' about it. This was *definitely* the stupidest thing he'd ever done.

Lose the jacket. Maybe the tie, too.

If only he'd told her the truth, right from the start . . . But she never would have agreed. No. This was the only way.

Keep the jacket. Lose the tie. Better.

Except Becca had always liked him in a tie. The face in the mirror glared at him now, accusing. What about Becca? And Amy. He didn't want to think about them, about everything that might have been. So much lost because of him. And now . . . what gave him the right to even think about trying again?

Dropping the tie into a drawer, Gren turned his back on the face in the mirror. It was almost eight, but not too late to call it all off. He crossed the room, jerked open the door, and strode down the hallway to the kitchen.

The room was spotless, no crumbs on the table, not a dish out of place, even though Nikki had spent most of the day preparing dinner. For him. No. He couldn't call things off. Not now. Not after she'd worked so hard.

She was nowhere to be seen at the moment, but he could hear her moving around upstairs, tucking the sprout into bed, getting ready, putting on a dress . . . Good grief, had he really said that? And survived? The woman was full of surprises. And her dinner, baking slowly in the oven, smelled absolutely delicious. His mouth was beginning to water.

Gren pushed the screen door open and stepped out onto the porch, into a soft grey dusk. It would be dark soon, and it really was too late. One way or another, this dinner was going to happen. And Nikki was absolutely right. He was nervous. He couldn't remember the last time he'd felt this way — heart racing, mouth dry, palms sweating — a lot like a man who'd just dug his own grave. He planted himself on the top step and lifted his face to the cool evening breeze. Breathing the peppery-sweet scent of ripe corn, he closed his eyes and tried not to think beyond the next minute, beyond the chirp of crickets, the rustle of leaves, and the measured, relentless pounding of his own heart.

'She's late.'

Gren shot to his feet and turned to face her. He looked surprised, she thought, and nervous, and very different with his hair combed and all that stubble shaved off his chin. No frayed blue jeans tonight, either, but a comfortable-looking tweed jacket over a navy blue shirt and pants. Noble would probably say he'd 'cleaned up real good'. She smiled. The bare feet were an interesting touch. What would his special someone think about that?

Nikki let her forehead rest against the screen door and waited for him to say something. It was a long wait. She tried again.

'You don't think she's lost . . . '

'Uh, no. I . . . I'm sure she's not lost.'

He didn't sound sure at all. 'Well, good. Guess I should check on the salmon.'

The screen door squeaked open as she turned away, and Gren followed her across the kitchen. 'Looks about done,' she said, tapping the crust with her knuckle. The heat from the oven felt good on her bare arms and face, and she lingered for a moment. Strange how the weather had suddenly turned so cold.

'Nikki?'

She closed the oven and straightened — a little too quickly. Gren caught her arm.

'Are you all right?'

Her eyes were playing tricks on her now. For just a moment, she thought she saw two Gren Wilders peering down at her. Both of them looked way too concerned. 'I'm fine.' She blinked the extra Gren away and smiled. 'Why?'

'You look . . . pale. Very nice, but pale.'

Very nice? 'I'm always pale.' She brushed his hand away, wrapping her arms around herself. 'Is it cold in here?'

'Cold?'

'Should I put the salad out? Or — maybe you don't want to eat right away. I'll wait till she gets here.'

'Uh, well . . . truth is, she's already here.'

'*What?*' She looked past him, into the dining room. Empty. 'She's here? Where? Shouldn't you be — '

Gren was staring at his toes, hands in his pockets, looking thoroughly uncomfortable. What on earth . . . *Oh, no!* Her gaze flew to the door at the other end of the room, the door to his office, his bedroom, then back to his face. He looked up and shrugged, gave a sheepish little smile.

'Oh! I . . . I'm sorry. I'll just . . . I'll go back upstairs until . . . '

'What?'

He caught her by the hand and held tight. 'Why would you — ' His gaze followed hers to the door at the end of the room. 'Oh, no.' Laughing, he held her hand a little tighter.

What the heck was so funny? No way was she serving them dinner in bed. Nikki tried to pull away.

'Boy, have you got the wrong idea.'

'Oh yeah?' She tried again to escape, but Gren held fast, his thumb tracing a slow circle on the back of her hand. Somebody sure had the wrong idea, and he wasn't laughing anymore.

She watched his thumb move slowly across her skin and felt herself shiver. It was just the cold night air, though, not the touch. *Right.* 'What wrong idea is that?'

'She's here.'

She glanced at the door again. 'So you said. But I — '

'No. *Right here.*' Gren caught her other hand in his and stepped closer.

Oh, God, the man even smelled good tonight. Nikki stared at the neat row of buttons on the front of his shirt and tried to hold her breath. *Right here?* This couldn't be happening.

The buttons moved closer.

'Dinner smells wonderful,' he said quietly. 'Are you hungry?'

Six buttons. She followed them up to his chin, to that playfully crooked grin. 'Me?' The word tumbled out on a rush of pent-up breath. How stupid had that sounded? She was probably blushing, too. *Dammit!*

'Don't be angry.' His grin faded. 'You did promise me a perfect dinner, remember?'

Me. She remembered. But this was all so new . . . the way his hands held hers, strong but gentle, a perfect fit. The way he looked at her, with eyes so full of promise, warm and reassuring. And his lips . . .

'Nikki?'

'I d-don't . . . I don't know what to say.' And that was the truth. She probably should be angry. Or something.

'Say yes. Say I'm hungry. And go sit down. You've done more than enough work for one day.'

'But — '

'No buts. You did all the hard stuff. I think I can take it from here.'

She let him lead her into the dining room, sank onto the chair when he pulled it out from the table, and stared up at him, still speechless and feeling . . . well, she wasn't quite sure what she was feeling. But it wasn't entirely unpleasant.

'Would you like some wine?'

He struck a match, lit the trio of candles she'd placed in the center of the table, and then grinned. 'I got both kinds . . . '

She drew an arid little breath. Definitely not angry. When had her mouth gotten so dry? 'Wine would be nice.' A laugh bubbled out of nowhere before she could finish the thought. 'Red please.'

He groaned. 'Went through all that for nothing, did I?'

'Fraid so.'

Gren filled her glass without spilling a drop. Surprising, because his gaze didn't stray from her face the whole time.

'You'll like it,' he said quietly. 'It's Greek . . . my favorite.'

Nikki lifted the glass to her lips and took a single sip. 'Mmmmm. That is good. Pretty, too.' It sparkled in the candlelight, an odd mix of ruby and amber. But Gren wasn't looking at the wine. He was watching her and looking . . . hungry. She wished he'd stop, wished she dared take another sip of wine, too, but suddenly remembered the aspirin she'd swallowed before she came downstairs. Wine and aspirin. Bad idea. Especially on an empty stomach.

'Where are you going?' Gren caught her hand again the moment she stood up, then dropped it the instant she looked down. Too bad. She was starting to like the feeling.

'I need a sweater. Be right back.'

'Oh, no you don't. You'll wake up the

sprout. And much as I love Claire, she is *not* invited to this meal.'

Suddenly weak-kneed, Nikki sank onto her chair. *I love Claire.* 'I'll be very quiet.'

'Uh-uh. Stay put. I'll find something.'

I love Claire. He was back before she had time to process that rather amazing statement, draping a warm, bulky sweater around her shoulders. It was grey, soft and just a little threadbare. All the buttons were missing. And it smelled good. Like him. She shrugged it on, wrapped it close around her and closed her eyes. Sandalwood, sharp and sweet, like wrapping herself in his arms.

'You sure you're all right?'

She shivered again as his fingers brushed her cheek. 'I'm fine.' *You're losing your mind!*

'You feel very warm.'

'Not warm, cold. But the sweater's nice.' *Very nice.* 'Thanks.'

'I'll go get our dinner.'

'You should — '

214

He stopped in the doorway and scowled at her.

'Right. I forgot. You're going to take it from here.'

'Now you've got it. Enjoy your wine.'

Nikki pushed the glass away, then turned to watch him at work in the kitchen. It was slowly sinking in. She was the special someone he was so anxious to impress. She was the one who'd turned him into a bundle of nerves this morning. Now it was her turn. Good grief, her hands were actually trembling. Uh-uh. No way! It was just another shiver. The sweater hadn't warmed her up yet, that was all.

She smoothed the front of her dress, checked that she hadn't missed any buttons. Fifty of them, at least, marching all the way down the front from neck to hem. The dress was long — too long? Plain black with short, cap sleeves. It made her look . . . capable. For just an instant, she let herself remember Gastown, the days of shaggy red hair and eyebrow rings. What would

Gren Wilder think of that? she wondered. Staring down at her feet, at the sensible black shoes laced up to the ankles, she sighed. What on earth did the man see in her?

'Lose something?'

'What?' Nikki jerked upright, watched him place two perfect plates of salad on the table. 'Uh, no ... I was just ...' She looked down at his feet and grinned. 'Just thinking I might take my shoes off, too.'

'Oh.' He looked down, frowned as if he hadn't noticed the bare feet until that very minute, and shook his head. 'I had the feeling I'd forgotten something.'

'You mean you —'

He winked, then pointed at the pale blue violets she'd sprinkled across the top of the salad and wrinkled his nose. 'Are we supposed to eat those?'

'Well, they are edible. Pretty good, too. But you don't have to. Just eat —'

'What you like.' He smiled as they finished the sentence together. 'Looks almost too good to eat, though. Don't you think?'

'I used to work with a chef who called his food edible art.'

'Mmmmm. I'd say this qualifies. Where was that?'

She stopped herself just short of blurting out the truth. Vancouver. Was that what this was all about? Another fishing expedition? The thought shivered its way through her body, setting her hand a-tremble as she reached for her fork.

He was watching. Munching on salad, little blue violets and all, and watching. What if all he wanted was a story? Say something!

'Out west.' She moved the food around her plate, waiting, trying to avoid looking at him. *Don't ask. Don't push it. Oh, please, don't spoil this.*

'Out west?' He put the fork down, sipped his wine, and grinned at her. 'Are we talking Brampton or . . . y'know, Minsk?'

She smiled in spite of herself. 'Not

that west.' Maybe he wasn't fishing, after all. Maybe it was just pleasant conversation. Wasn't that what people did over dinner? Normal people anyway. Too bad she wasn't normal people. She couldn't even remember how to fake it anymore. 'Does it matter?'

Gren sighed. 'No. It doesn't matter. I just thought . . . never mind.' He finished chewing and pushed his plate away. 'You're not eating. Should I be worried?'

'Worried?' She looked up, saw two of him again, and felt strangely light-headed.

'Well, y'know what they say. When the cook won't eat . . . '

Nikki gripped the edge of the table and held on as the room swam around her.

'Nikki?'

His voice sounded hollow, far away and echoey. And there were three of him now . . . or four. She shivered again and couldn't stop. Something was very,

very wrong. 'Gren . . . '

He . . . *they* were moving, a shimmering, fluid group across the table, then close beside her, breath cold against her cheek. Was he saying something? The room pitched again.

'I think . . . I'm . . . sick.'

'I think you're right. Nikki, you're burning up.'

'Oh, no . . . Claire.' She lurched to her feet, or tried to. Gren caught her as the walls fell away. She couldn't feel the floor beneath her feet, only his arms around her. Her world and everything in it was spinning, out of control. She had to find Claire.

'Don't fight me.'

'Claire . . . I have to . . . '

'No. Nikki! *Think about it*. You're not going anywhere near Claire with this fever.'

'But . . . she might be s-sick, too.'

'I'll check on her. I promise.'

'Gren?' She was falling now. No. His arms were still around her, still holding her safe. She could feel his tweed

219

jacket, cold and scratchy against her cheek. Maybe they were both falling. She tried to hold on, but only slipped farther and farther away.

'It's all right now. You can let go.'

She opened her eyes, searched the light for his face. 'Where . . . '

'You're in my room.'

'Your . . . ' No. This was wrong. She couldn't be so helpless, so confused. What was she doing in his room, his bed? The air felt cold in her lungs, the sheets and pillow like ice against her skin. 'Claire?'

His fingers brushed gently across her face and through her hair. 'I'm going to go check on her now. You stay put, okay?'

She tried to move, tried to focus on his face. She wasn't going anywhere. 'You have to take c-care of her. P-please, Gren.'

'I promise.'

'But you . . . you d-don't understand.'

'You can tell me all about it in the morning.'

'N-no. They might . . . ' She caught his hand and held on. 'Don't let them hurt her.' Those few words took the last of her strength. She couldn't really see him anymore, but she could feel him, still holding her hand. And she could hear his voice, soft and gentle, from very far away. She tried to hold onto the voice, tried to believe what it was saying.

'You can trust me.'

What choice did she have?

11

'She's almost asleep, the little sweetie. Sure does like you, doesn't she?' Aprile draped one arm around his shoulders and gave a sisterly squeeze. 'Put her down now, Gren. Take her upstairs to bed.'

Claire snuggled even closer, nestling her face into the hollow of his neck, catching a fistful of hair with one tiny hand. Aprile had it right this time. And the feeling was undeniably mutual.

'How's Nikki?'

She didn't answer. Gren's throat tightened as he turned to face her, fighting an unexpected, almost painful, surge of panic. 'Aprile?'

She was grinning. Great. Up to her old tricks again. Probably thought she'd discovered some deep, hidden meaning behind his simple question. He frowned. 'Well?'

222

'Dead to the world.'

'Poor choice of words, sis.' He stroked Claire's back, tried to make himself relax, willing his heart to stop pounding. Nikki was fine. She had to be. He'd made her a promise about that. Come to think of it, he'd made her a whole lot of promises last night . . .

'She'll be just fine,' said Aprile at last. 'Doc says he's seen half a dozen people with this virus in the last couple of weeks. Hits hard and fast, but doesn't last long.' She patted his arm, a comfortably familiar touch. 'Her fever broke a while ago. I expect she'll sleep all day — this one's got her beat.'

You don't know Nikki. His moment of panic vanished on a sigh of relief. She really was okay, thank God. And if he hadn't forgotten how to pray, he might do exactly that.

Instead, he looked down at Claire, held her a bit closer, resting his cheek against her forehead. Her skin still felt cool. Maybe it was time he tried remembering one of those prayers. He couldn't bear the thought of this tiny sprout of a person having to suffer what Nikki had endured in the last eighteen hours.

Aprile laughed. 'Oh, boy, have you got it bad!'

'Huh?' He scowled a warning at her. 'What's that supposed to mean?'

'The short version?'

'You can do that?'

She scowled back. 'Very funny. Short version . . . I told you so.'

'Told me what?' As if he didn't know.

'That our Nikki is perfect for you.'

Ugh. The only thing worse than a sisterly 'I told you so', was knowing the 'I told you so' was right. Well, maybe one thing worse. *She* could know she was right. For now, at least, she was still guessing. *Keep it that way!* Gren gave a skeptical shrug. 'I hardly know her.'

'Mmm-hmm. And that romantic little dinner for two . . . '

'It was just dinner. Seemed like a good idea. I thought if we got to know each other, she might relax.'

'Ah, relax. And then fall in love with you, maybe?'

'No. Relax and tell me what she's so afraid of.'

'Afraid?'

'She's hiding something, Aprile. Running from something. And I intend to find out what it is.'

Aprile seemed to be considering the possibilities, lips pursed, thin black eyebrows knit together. 'I don't know, Gren. I think you're imagining things. Looking for a story under every rock, as usual. Just leave the poor girl alone — well, except for the getting to know her part, that is.'

Gren ignored his sister's sly wink. 'I'm not imagining anything. Not this time. She hovers over the sprout like . . . like a worried mama bear, always checking over her shoulder, testing the wind. Always . . . '

She looked skeptical. 'Always what?'

'Well, the other night for instance. She was out somewhere when I came home, and when she got back . . . '

Aprile folded her arms and stared at him, tap-foot impatient already. 'Well? When she got back . . . *what?* For heaven's sake Grenville, spit it out.'

What was the point? She was in no mood to believe him anyway. He shrugged again. 'You're right. It was probably nothing.'

'Thought you were going to tell me she'd clobbered you again.'

'Huh. Not this time.'

Claire interrupted with a sleepy sigh, tucking her thumb into her mouth.

'We'll talk about it later. I'd better get the sprout into bed. She's about to conk out — what a grip!' The handful of hair she'd laid claim to was now a tightly twisted knot. Like mother like daughter, thought Gren. Seemed they both knew how to give a man a headache.

'Good idea,' said Aprile, slipping into her 'sister knows best' voice. 'And then get some rest yourself. You look beat.'

Uh-oh, lecture time. 'I'm okay.'

'Now, Gren, you really should — '

'Sis?'

She stopped, looked expectantly up at him. In the old days, she would've bulldozed right over an interruption like that one. He wasn't about to give her a chance to change her mind. 'Don't start with me, okay? I don't want to go to sleep. Not right now, anyway.'

She shrugged. It was one of those 'you'll be sorry and I'm going to say I told you so' shrugs he'd been enduring all his life.

'Maybe I'll sit with Nikki for a while.' There. That ought to pacify her.

'Suit yourself.' She punctuated the comment with an indignant sniff, but Gren was certain he saw her mouth twitch — the merest hint of a smile.

'Guess I'll just clean up,' she said, 'and then, if Nikki's still asleep, I may lie down for a while myself.'

He studied her face for a moment. She did look tired. And it wasn't just the lack of makeup — a condition that, for the life of him, he couldn't remember encountering before. She must've been getting ready for bed when he called last night, but had instead come rushing to his rescue. Now her usually bright eyes were almost painfully heavy-lidded. Big sister had really come through for him, again. Wouldn't hurt to tell her so. 'I, uh . . . '

'What now?'

'Nothing. Just . . . thanks.'

She smiled, crossing the room to give him another hug, adding a quick kiss on the cheek this time. 'You're welcome. What for?'

'For everything . . . Driving all the way out here in the middle of the night, calling the doctor, taking care of Nikki . . . I owe you one.'

Aprile laughed, a throaty, satisfied chuckle. 'It's not all that far to drive, Grenville. And if you hadn't been in such a panic, you'd have thought to call the doctor yourself.' She patted his arm, then gently smoothed Claire's hair. 'I'll always be there for you. You know that, right?'

He nodded.

'Take the poor child up to bed. And Gren?'

'Mmmmm?'

'You owe me a couple of dozen.'

Great. Just great. He could hear Aprile rattling dishes, still chuckling away to herself as he climbed the stairs and settled the sprout into her crib. He was going to pay dearly for this, probably for the rest of his life. And there was no way around it. *Nikki is perfect for you.* Damned if the woman wasn't right.

As Claire's dark eyes drifted slowly shut, he straightened the blanket, tucked her old rag doll in beside her, and bent to kiss her cheek. She made a low, contented gurgle. For a long, peaceful moment, Gren stood quietly, watching her sleep. Strange how things had changed. He'd been almost afraid of her at first. But now . . . taking care of her, loving her, felt as natural, as right, as anything he'd ever done.

'Sweet dreams, Sprout. I'll keep you safe. You and your mom. I promise.'

★ ★ ★

The blankets felt heavy. Almost as heavy as the thing on her head. What was that, anyway? A pillow? It was cold and damp.

Nikki tried to move, tried to lift one arm and brush the thing away, but suddenly her body felt heavy, too. A quick, deep breath burned in her lungs. What was that funny smell? Pungent, strangely sour, something she couldn't quite . . .

She clutched at the blankets, fighting a wave of panic and confusion. *Hang on. Don't give in to it.* She gulped another sharp breath. Maybe she was dreaming. Yes, that had to be it. She was dreaming. Or dead, said a frightened little voice inside her head. No. *Find out! Open your eyes.*

But her eyes didn't want to be open. She forced one, halfway, and recoiled from a painfully bright light. *Not dreaming*. Sunlight? She must've forgotten to close the drapes last night, or . . .

Hesitant, now, to trust her senses, she unclenched her hands and willed them away from her body. It felt as if she was dragging a couple of weights at the ends of her arms. The sheets seemed to go on forever, and felt like sandpaper beneath her fingers. But that wasn't right . . . This couldn't be the little cot in Claire's nursery. This was — *Claire?!*

Her eyes flew open. She groaned, squinting into the light, searching for something, anything familiar. Where was Claire?

With that thought, the night came back in a rush of comprehension . . . the awful headache that had plagued her all day yesterday, the astonishing truth about Gren's dinner for two and his 'special someone', the cold, dizzy feeling, the double vision, and then falling, falling . . .

You're in my room. His room. His

231

bed. *You're not going anywhere near Claire with this fever.*

Now she remembered. She'd made him promise, begged him to keep the baby safe. *Don't let them hurt her.* But what else had she said? What else had she told him?

You can trust me. She could almost hear his voice again, gentle and faraway, as he tried to make her believe. But beyond that moment her mind was a frightening void. Had it really happened just last night? Or were those random scraps of memory left over from days ago? For all she knew, she'd been sick for a very long time. It felt that way. Everything hurt — skin, muscle, even her hair — a dull, constant ache that seemed to grow teeth when she moved . . . as if something had crept inside of her and sharpened her bones.

And now someone was moaning, low and mournful, almost a feeling more than a sound. It couldn't be Claire, could it? Was she sick too? Gren had promised he'd look after the baby. He'd promised nothing bad would happen to her. That much she remembered. But he hadn't been able to promise she'd never get sick.

That moaning again. What . . . It took a few moments to grasp the fact that the sound was coming from her, from somewhere deep inside. Was she really that helpless, that out of control? *Make it stop!* She tried to hold her breath.

'Nikki?'

A gentle hand brushed her hair, lifted the weight from her forehead — not a pillow after all, but a damp cloth, meant to soothe the fever. A warm, dry hand took its place. Gren's hand.

'Nikki, can you hear me?'

'Mmmmm.' She held onto his voice, tried to focus on his face. She had to know. 'C-Claire?' Her voice trembled — a voice she barely recognized — little more than a hoarse whisper.

'She's fine. Sound asleep right now.'

'Are you s-sure?' She tried to swallow, brushed her dry tongue across parched lips, and croaked another few words. 'She's not . . . sick?'

His hand moved gently across her brow. 'I'm sure. Just put her down for her nap a few minutes ago. Here, you should drink. Try a sip of water.'

Nikki let him lift her head off the pillow, let him hold the glass to her lips. It felt strange to be so dependent, stranger still to have someone to depend on. Strange . . . and wonderful.

'Thanks.'

'Don't try to talk, okay?' His thumb brushed a dribble of water away from her chin. 'Just rest. I'll stay right here.'

'But — '

'Shhhh. Stop worrying. When the sprout wakes up, we'll hear her. I brought the nursery monitor with me, see?'

Her eyes wouldn't focus on the object in his hand. Nikki settled on his face instead. He looked so tired. 'How . . . how long have I been . . . '

'Since last night. Eighteen, maybe nineteen hours now. But the worst is over. Doc says you'll be back in business in no time.' Gren settled himself in the chair, folding his arms across his chest, propping his feet on the end of the bed. 'Now stop talking.'

Doc says? She let her eyes fall shut. It was so hard to concentrate. And she didn't remember seeing the doctor. She didn't remember *anything*. 'Gren?'

'I'm right here.' His voice sounded sleepy.

'What's that funny smell?'

'Funny smell? She heard the chair squeak as he sat up. 'Uh, well ... probably this stuff. Witch hazel. Doc said a sponge bath would help bring the fever down.' The chair squeaked again. 'Try to sleep, okay?'

Sponge bath? Nikki kept her eyes closed tight as she groped around under the covers, searching for the familiar row of buttons on the front of her dress. No buttons. Suddenly her mouth felt very dry again. She lifted the covers and opened one eye. No dress. In its place was a wrinkled grey T-shirt, at least three sizes too big.

His room, his bed, his clothes . . . and still she couldn't remember. She dropped the covers and squeezed her eyes shut.

'Don't worry,' said Gren in a drowsy voice. 'The sponge bath was Aprile's department, not mine.'

She didn't have to open her eyes to know he was wearing that crooked grin again, she could hear it in his voice. 'Aprile?'

'Mmm-hmm. Drove out last night. Figured I might need some help.'

'Is she still here?'

'Mmm-hmm. Long as we need her.'

'That's so nice — '

'Shhhhh. You need . . . to rest.'

More like you need to rest, thought Nikki, curling onto her side. It was a slow, awkward process, one stiff, stubborn muscle at a time. A little less painful now, though. And the fog was slowly lifting from her mind.

Who wants to hurt you, Nikki? Who wants to hurt Claire? She could hear his voice just as clearly as when he'd asked those two questions last night. But how had she answered? What did he know?

For nearly half an hour she watched him sleep, watched the slow, steady rise and fall of his chest. It was almost hypnotic. His chair was empty when she finally woke up again, still wondering . . . what did he know?

12

'You shouldn't be up.'

Nikki frowned at him over the rim of her mug, savoring another sip of hot lemon tea before she replied. Slouched in his chair at the end of the kitchen table, heavy-eyed and absently stroking the shadow of beard on his chin, it seemed to her that Gren was the one who needed to get some rest. No point in saying so, though. He wouldn't listen. 'I'm feeling much better.'

'Maybe so, but — '

'But nothing. I was going stir crazy, just lying there staring at the ceiling. It's been a whole day.'

'The doctor said you should rest.'

'The doctor said I'd be better in no time.' She shrugged. 'Well, I'm better. Thanks to you and Aprile.'

Gren glanced up at her for a moment, took a deep breath as if about

238

to speak, then abruptly lowered his gaze to the table. What was he thinking? What would explain the sudden stiffening of his shoulders, the rigid set of his jaw?

'Gren?'

He didn't look up, just studied the tabletop, tracing the grain of the wood with one finger. 'Mmmm?'

'Is something wrong?'

The finger stopped. 'You tell me, Nikki.' He raised his head slowly as he spoke, meeting her gaze, expectant and unwavering. 'Is something wrong?'

Slowly, she lowered her mug of tea onto the table, lacing her fingers around it, holding tight, holding herself together. *Who wants to hurt you, Nikki? Who wants to hurt Claire?* She'd tried so hard to remember what she'd said to him — if she'd said anything at all. Silence on the subject of Frank Medici was so ingrained in her by now, she'd almost convinced herself she'd managed to hold her tongue. But things were bound to slip out in the throes of a fever — scraps of memory and confession, shreds of reality turned to nightmare. What if she'd spoken Frank's name? What if Gren knew?

Don't panic. This was not the time to fall apart. She tried to swallow but couldn't — couldn't even lift the mug of tea to moisten her lips. If only she'd stayed in bed. Far better to stare at the ceiling than to face the question in his eyes and have to answer with lies. 'I . . . I don't understand.'

Gren sighed. Folding his arms across his chest, he leaned back in his chair and let the silence grow between them. To Nikki it felt like a wall.

'Who did this to you?' he said at last. 'Who made it so impossible for you to trust me?'

He didn't know. 'But I do trust you.' The words tumbled out before she had a chance to consider what they might mean. Surprisingly, they were true. And, even more surprising, she wanted . . . no, *needed* him to believe. '*I do.*'

'Not enough to tell me the truth.'

No more lies. He deserved better than that. But how could she justify telling him things that might put his life in danger? 'Truth? About what?'

Gren stared at her for a long moment, then pushed away from the table and paced the room. 'About why you're here, hiding out. About who, or what, you're so afraid of. About — '

Behind him the staircase creaked, announcing Aprile's approach just seconds before she bustled through the kitchen door. 'Nikki, you're up! Well, good for you.'

Gren scowled. Shoving both hands into his pockets, he stared bleakly out the screen door.

Nikki breathed a sigh of relief for the moment's reprieve. 'Yes, and feeling much better. I can't thank you enough . . . '

'Don't worry yourself, my dear. I was more than glad to help.' Aprile poured a cup of tea and carried it to the table, glancing briefly at her brother before she sat. 'What's with him?'

'Well . . . ' Nikki looked up. Gren was watching, wearing a weary, wounded expression. He didn't speak, just nudged the door open and made his escape to the porch. She sighed again. 'Guess he thinks I should still be in bed.'

'Poor Gren. He was terribly worried about you, you know.' Aprile sipped her tea and smiled. 'Having you and little Claire in the house has done him a world of good.'

More like turned his world upside-down. 'I'm afraid we've been a lot of trouble.'

'No, Nikki, you've given him something to think about besides himself . . . besides the past. And I thank you for that.'

You wouldn't thank me if you knew.

'Be patient with him, won't you, dear? My brother is much too hard on himself sometimes. Understandable, I guess . . . Just don't take his moods to heart.' Aprile didn't wait for an answer, reaching across the table to pat Nikki's hand. 'He's smitten, I think. With you and your little one. And not quite sure what to do about it.'

Smitten? 'Aprile, I — '

'Oh, don't look so surprised! Even Noble says I'm right. As a matter of fact, he says it's mutual.' She laughed, ignoring Nikki's stammered objection. 'My dear, it's as plain as that darling little blush you're wearing, so don't even bother denying it. Now, I really must go — simply detest driving after dark. Your little angel is sound asleep already . . . such a sweetheart . . . '

Aprile stopped talking long enough to dash upstairs, reappearing a moment later with an overnight bag slung over her shoulder. ' . . . do take care of yourself, now. Don't work too hard. It's bound to take some time to feel all better, you know. And Nikki? Remember what I said. Bye now!'

The door slammed shut behind her, but Aprile kept right on talking, to her brother this time. 'You be sure she gets lots of rest, Grenville, and don't be neglecting yourself, either . . . '

'Bye now,' whispered Nikki, slightly breathless after Aprile's nonstop monologue. The two voices outside grew fainter, finally drowned out by the crunch of gravel underfoot as brother and sister strolled across the driveway. A car door slammed. In another minute or two Aprile would be gone and Gren would be back, wanting his answers.

She stretched, testing still-achy muscles before pushing to her feet. It seemed so unfair to avoid him after all he'd done. Maybe if he thought she'd gone back to bed . . .

Ignoring the prick of guilty conscience, Nikki climbed the stairs, forcing her stiff legs to hurry, and tiptoed into Claire's nursery for the first time in two unbearably long days. The first they'd ever been apart since that night in Gastown. She bent to kiss the baby's cheek. This was why she had to keep the past a secret. So that nothing and no one could ever hurt Claire.

Wasn't that exactly what Gren had promised? She turned to watch him out the window. While she couldn't remember anything at all of what she'd said to him during that feverish night, scraps of what he had said were beginning to come back to her. Not just questions, but promises. Whispered words about trust and faith. Even love. She remembered the soft brush of his hand on her cheek, his breath, cool against her skin, the touch of his lips.

Trust me. I won't ever let anyone hurt you or Claire. I promise.

Nikki watched from the window, long after Aprile's shiny black sedan had rounded the bend and disappeared from view. Gren lingered in the middle of the driveway, head down, arms folded across his chest. What was he waiting for? Why didn't he just —

Abruptly, he turned to look at the house. Nikki stepped away from the window, holding her breath, waiting for the slam of the screen door . . . It never came.

Careful to stay in the shadows, she moved back to the window, hiding herself in the green velvet folds of the curtain. Where was he? She saw him at last and gasped a painfully ragged breath. Instead of returning to the house, Gren had crossed the lawn and now stood in front of the old tool shed, one hand on the latch.

No! Her stomach turned in on itself as he pulled the door open. *Please, no . . .*

Glancing quickly over his shoulder, as if to be certain he hadn't been seen, he slipped inside.

Heart pounding, Nikki clutched at the drapery with both hands. What was he doing? Searching? She watched his shadowy form move back and forth beyond the dusty, mullioned window of the shed and knew she had to stop him. Another minute or two and it would be too late. If he found it before she had a chance to explain . . .

Suddenly lightheaded, she stumbled through the nursery door and down the stairs. Her legs, so stiff and achy just moments ago, felt like tired rubber bands as she made her way through the kitchen and across the yard, moving in painful slow motion. Breathless, she wrenched open the shed door. '*What are you doing?*'

The hammer Gren had been about to lift off its hook clattered to the floor, narrowly missing his toes. 'Good grief, Nikki . . . you scared me. Never mind what I'm doing, what the hell are *you* doing?'

She tottered unsteadily in the doorway, painfully aware of what she must look like to him — windblown, wild-eyed, completely out of breath. Completely out of her mind. 'I was . . . I just . . . just wanted to take a walk.' Still shaky, she sank onto a nearby packing crate, wrapping her arms around herself. 'Guess maybe . . . I overdid it, huh?'

Gren studied her for a long moment, then bent to pick up the hammer. 'Loose board,' he said quietly.

Her stomach lurched again.

'Oh?' It was all she could manage to say. She held herself a little tighter, longing to look down at the floor, at the worn pine plank with the notched corner, just steps from where he stood. Her perfect hiding place. Instead she focused on him, on his face, and the dark eyes that watched her so intently. Did he know? 'Loose b-board?'

'Mmm-hmm. In the . . . '

Nikki held her breath as he rummaged through a box of nails, finally selecting three that might do the job. *In the what?!* Wasn't he ever going to finish the sentence?

' . . . uh . . . dining room. Figured I'd better fix it, y'know, before the sprout starts walking around on her own.' He looked at her and frowned. 'You all right?'

I am now. 'Fine. Just a little winded.' She forced a smile. 'Are you heading back to the house?'

Still frowning, he dropped the nails into his shirt pocket, stepping closer, stepping away from the notched pine board. 'You did overdo it, didn't you? Need some help getting back inside?'

The smile came a little more easily this time. 'No, I'm fine. Stop fussing. You're as bad as Aprile.'

'Nobody's as bad as Aprile.' Despite his lighthearted tone, Gren remained solemnly straight-faced.

'Hmm. Whatever you say. I was just going to ask if you'd mind checking on Claire. She was sound asleep a couple of minutes ago, but I forgot to bring the monitor with me, and — '

'No problem. Aren't you coming in?'

'Soon. But it feels so good to breathe fresh air. I'd like to sit here for a while — just a bit longer.'

Gren seemed tense, she thought, almost awkward, as if he wanted to look away but wasn't able. When he finally broke eye contact, his gaze roamed around the shed, across the floor, and his somber expression grew doubtful. Watching, Nikki found herself holding her breath again. He couldn't know . . . could he?

'Well . . . if you're sure. But take it easy, okay?' Turning away as he spoke, Gren strode slowly across the lawn, fist clenched around the hammer head.

When he paused to look back at her from the top step, Nikki raised her hand and nodded, tried her best to smile, but his darkly troubled manner left her fighting an equally dark and troubling panic. Was this more than just misplaced concern for her health? Had he discovered the secrets hidden beneath the pine board? One more minute and she'd know for sure.

So that's what brought her running. Gren snugged the soft, pink blanket around Claire's shoulders and moved quietly to the window. She must've been up here, checking on the sprout. A glance outside at just the right moment and she would've seen him go into the shed. Pure luck that she hadn't caught him with his nose in that old gym bag. Then again, maybe it wasn't so lucky. If she'd caught him, it might have forced her hand. She might have been willing to explain.

He leaned heavily against the windowsill, watching as Nikki hauled herself up off the crate and disappeared into the gloomy interior of the tool shed. It didn't matter. He didn't need to see her to know she'd be on her hands and knees by now, pulling up that loose board at the end of the workbench, lifting layer after layer of dusty, yellowed newspaper, coaxing open a stubborn zipper . . .

Slipping two fingers into the back pocket of his jeans, he extracted the lone item he'd dared to take from the bag and studied it thoughtfully. A computer disk. Not the answer he'd sought. No, quite the opposite. This was a whole new set of questions.

★ ★ ★

Nikki pried up the notched pine board and tossed it aside, desperate to know if her secrets — Lainey's secrets

— were still safe.

You were right about Frank. Why didn't I listen?

She could almost hear her sister's voice again, nervous and halting. A few dozen words on an answering machine. Last words.

Doesn't matter. I'm doing something about it now.

Her hands shook as she peeled off the layers of newspaper. Brittle and yellowed, the sheets tore apart beneath her frantic fingers. If only she'd been there to answer that last phone call. It might have made a difference. Lainey might still be alive.

He doesn't know about you, Cat. You're the only one who can keep my baby safe.

Safe! Nikki breathed a shuddering sigh. It was still there, just as she'd left it. Grabbing the worn, canvas straps with both hands, she hauled the heavy gym bag out of the hole and dropped it onto the floor beside her. The zipper stuck once, twice, a little rusty after eight long months in the damp earth. Trembling, she forced it open and peered inside.

The money is for her . . . for her future.

The money. Frank's money. She hated the look of it, even the smell of it. She'd never been able to bring herself to count, but it had to be a lot. At least fifty thousand dollars, all tens and twenties. For Claire? That was something else she couldn't stomach. In all their months of hiding, even through that seemingly endless trek across the country, she hadn't spent one penny of Frank Medici's dirty money. With luck, she never would.

And the disk . . . that's your insurance.

Nikki touched the plastic case, finally picking it up, turning it over and over in her hands. No. She wouldn't open it. Wouldn't get any closer to Frank Medici than she had to.

Frank won't want it to get out. You'll know when the time comes to use it.

Till then, just hang on.

When the time comes to use it . . . Forget luck. Maybe the time to use it was now. Maybe all she had to do was tell Gren and ask for his help. Surely with all his newspaper connections, he'd know people . . . people who might be able to help them straighten things out.

It's too late for me. I'm already dead. It's all up to you now.

Nikki shoved the bag back into the hole, feeling strangely calm all of a sudden, as if the decision to tell Gren had been inevitable, and right. Thank goodness he hadn't discovered anything on his own. It was bad enough knowing he suspected her of hiding something. She couldn't bear to imagine what he'd think of a bag full of money buried in the shed — what he'd think of her because of it.

She stopped to examine the slim plastic case once again, then dropped it into the bag, unopened. Tugging impatiently on the zipper, hurriedly replacing the layers of newspaper and finally the notched pine board, she carefully hid all traces of Lainey's 'insurance'. The money could rot there for all she cared. And as for the disk . . . That would be up to Gren. Still, she couldn't help thinking it might be better, safer, if nobody ever looked at it again, if nobody ever tried to unlock its secrets.

13

'What do you see out there, pumpkin?'

Tired of playing zoo with Noble's handmade collection of wooden animals, Claire had spent the last few minutes watching the world through the kitchen door, her tiny nose pressed against the screen. Nikki scooped her off the floor and held her close. A hug was exactly what the two of them needed right about now. That, and maybe a call from Gren.

She glanced at the silent telephone and sighed. If only she'd told him the truth when she had the chance. She'd made the decision and marched straight back to the house, even practiced what she'd say to him on the way, but then . . .

Smiling at the memory, Nikki rested her forehead against Claire's and hugged the child a bit tighter.

'Remember that yummy soup Gren made for our dinner the other night?' Soup and a grilled cheese sandwich, golden brown and melting, just the way she liked it. Not exactly gourmet fare but, to Nikki, the simple meal had seemed ambrosian.

Afterwards, he'd sent her off to bed with a cup of hot lemon tea and a romantic novel. He'd been so thoughtful, so attentive, probably hoping that a little tender loving care would weaken her resolve, convince her to give in and tell all. In truth, his plan had almost worked. But when the moment came she'd been unwilling to spoil the mood, unwilling to burden him with a blunt confession and dangerous talk of Frank Medici. Morning would be soon enough, she'd told herself. In the morning she would tell him everything.

But by morning, Gren was gone.

'Ga-ga,' said Claire, beginning to squirm in Nikki's arms.

'I know, sweetie. I miss him, too.'

Claire struggled again. '*Ga-ga, Ga-ga!*'

'Oh . . . uh, right.' Feeling more than a little foolish, Nikki bent to pick Raggedy Man off the floor. The baby seemed to be coping with Gren's absence a lot better than the grown-up this time around. Unfortunately, the baby was in no mood to commiserate.

'No hugs? I have juice . . . and tickles!'

'*Naaaaaahh!*'

Huh. Even bribery wasn't going to do the trick. She filled a bottle with apple juice and settled Claire into her highchair. 'There you go, sweetie. Just the way you like it. But you still owe me one big hug.'

Turning, Nikki surveyed the jumble of books and paper littering the kitchen table. After seven months of *Minute Meals*, finding at least one new and interesting menu item every week was becoming a bit of a challenge. It was a challenge she enjoyed, though, and her customers were constantly amazed

— and pleasantly surprised — by the endless variety. Next up, an authentic Acadian Rappie Pie.

One-by-one, she gathered the Wilder family cookbooks into the crook of her arm and carefully returned them to their shelf. One of these days, she'd have to tell Gren she'd been tempting the palates of Vinegar Hill with some of his own great-grandmother's recipes. Would it please him? she wondered, tacking the shopping list onto the fridge with a well-worn strawberry magnet.

Beside it, stuck under a faded peach, was a rumpled scrap of paper — a note from Gren, written early yesterday morning and left in the center of the pine table for her to find. She read it again.

Taking you at your word that you're feeling better. Something came up at the paper — can't wait — and I may be gone for a while. Do us all a favor and take it easy, okay? Hug Claire for me. Gren

'I would if she'd let me,' muttered

Nikki, pulling the note off the fridge and crumpling it in her hand as she crossed the room. This time, she really would throw it away. Or maybe not. Good grief! It was just a piece of paper, a few hastily scribbled words. But somehow the note felt like a part of him, a physical connection she wasn't ready to break.

Smoothing out the wrinkles, she shoved it back under the peach, beginning to wonder if maybe — *just maybe* — Noble and Aprile had been right all along. How else could she explain all this silly, sentimental behavior? She sighed, gazing wistfully out the window, feeling foolish all over again. How could she possibly miss him already? This love-stuff was going to take a whole lot of getting used to.

*   *   *

Gren paced the length of Harry May's seventh floor cubicle — all four-and-a-half short steps of it — for what seemed like the hundredth time. '*Well?*'

'Lists.' Harry dropped his glasses onto the desk. 'Two of them. Numbers and names.' Leaning back in his chair, he folded his hands behind his head, crossed his feet on the desktop, and yawned widely.

'Pretty impressive work, Harry. Guess that's why they pay you the big bucks, huh?'

As usual, Harry ignored the sarcasm. 'Hey, man, you asked what was on the disk. I told you. Lists.'

Gren glanced up at the all-too-familiar hand-printed page tacked to the wall above Harry's head. ASK THE RIGHT QUESTION. He muttered a curse. Apparently some things hadn't changed in the six years he'd been away. Reaching across the desk, he gave the man's feet a shove.

'Hey!' Harry's high-tops hit the floor with a thud as his chair jerked upright. 'What'd you do that for?'

'This one's personal, Harry. And I don't have a lot of time to waste. The list part I figured out on my own. Names and numbers. *But what do they mean? Anything ring a bell?'*

'Oh,' said Harry, parking his glasses on the end of his nose again as he turned back to the computer. 'Why didn't you say so? Gimme a minute.'

'Uh-huh.'

Numbers, names, and a sack full of money. What was Nikki up to? Gren paced the floor again, nervously clenching and unclenching his fists, uncomfortably aware that if it were anyone else, he wouldn't be wondering. He'd be telling himself it had to be criminal.

Why was he so quick to rule that out in her case? After all, he still knew next to nothing about the woman . . . except for the most important thing, of course — that he'd fallen in love with her, and with Claire, and it was far too late to change that fact, no matter what sort of trouble the two of them might be in.

He stopped pacing for a moment to watch Harry at work, hunched over the keyboard, chewing on a fingernail as he scrolled through the lists. Numbers and names. What were the chances that anything on either list would strike a familiar chord, even for self-proclaimed research king, Harry May? One in a million, if that.

Turning his back, Gren leaned wearily against the desk, folding his arms across his chest and closing his eyes. He remembered how nervous Nikki had been the night of their interrupted dinner, how her hands had trembled when he'd held them, how she'd smiled at him across the table, then clung to him later, begging him to take care of Claire, to protect her. She'd said something else, too. Something about a hiding place.

That was when he'd started making promises — he'd take care of them, make sure they'd both be safe, forever and always. Desperate to keep her hanging on through that awful fever, he'd even said something reckless about love, and family, and starting over . . . together.

He figured she'd confide in him after he'd bared himself like that, poured out all his hopes and dreams and all those new found emotions. She would finally have to believe she could trust him. But once it was over, she'd been just as distant, as suspiciously cautious, as ever. That was when he started thinking about the hiding place. He never would've found it if he hadn't been looking for some way to avoid going back into the house after Aprile left. He knew Nikki wasn't ready to talk about things, and couldn't bring himself to confront her, not when she still seemed so fragile and weak, so he went for a walk instead, through the garden, across the lawn, past the tool shed . . .

Once upon a time, he'd had a hiding place of his own in that old shed, a place to put things where Aprile wouldn't find them and tease him, or claim them for her own. Over the years he'd hidden countless trout flies, all painstakingly tied with Noble's help, workbooks crammed with notes about his latest 'investigation' — most often some made-up mystery involving big sister and some of her friends, his first pack of cigarettes, even those magazines Mom didn't approve of. It had to be twenty years since he'd thought of that hole in the floor. Nostalgia wasn't his thing. Too many pitfalls, too many unhappy memories waiting to pick away at his conscience. But he decided to check it out anyway. The way things had been going, that old hole in the floor just might be good for a laugh.

Gren heaved a frustrated sigh. He hadn't done much laughing in the last few days.

'*Ah-ha!*' Harry spun the chair around and shoved off with both feet, rolling full tilt to the far side of the cubicle. Grabbing a binder off the shelf, he wheeled back to his desk and flipped through the pages. '*Yes!* That's got to be it. Take a look. Here, see the numbers on the screen? Six or seven digits followed by a letter or two, right?'

Gren squinted at the monitor. 'Right, but — '

'But what do the letters mean? Exactly!' Harry pointed at the open page in front of him. 'Eight-three-three-two-oh-one-Ontario-Limited.' His finger stabbed the paper with every word. 'They're corporations, man. Numbered companies. Don't you see? The letter stands for the province of registry. 'O' for Ontario, 'A' for Alberta, 'M' for — well, you catch my drift. Whoo-eee! Look at 'em all! And I'll bet the names on the other list correlate.'

'Maybe,' said Gren, feeling nowhere near as enthusiastic as Harry seemed to be. Numbered corporations and buried money? He was getting a bad feeling about all of this. A *very* bad feeling. 'Recognize any of the names?'

'What d'you mean do I recognize any? Don't you, man?' Harry looked up at him, gaping in open-mouthed astonishment. His surprise lasted less than a second. 'Oh. Right. You've been . . . uh . . . away. Sorry.'

'Forget it. Just fill me in.'

'Right.' Harry traced a line down the computer screen with his finger. 'Never heard of these first few, but this one . . . Now, this one's a biggie. Turns up over and over, too.' He frowned, lowering his voice to a whisper. 'Frank Medici. Where'd you say you got this disk?'

'I didn't,' said Gren. 'Who's Medici?'

'Only one of the baddest of the bad guys. And keep your voice down.' Quickly, Harry popped the disk out of the drive and handed it across the desk, then wiped the file off his screen. 'Listen, Wilder, I know crime was never your regular beat, but you just might've lucked onto something. Something a lot of the other Clark Kent-types around here would be very interested in seeing, if you catch my drift.'

'I'm beginning to. What can you tell me about this Medici?'

'Shhhh!' hissed Harry, glancing nervously around the tiny room as if wishing he had a door to slam, and maybe a lock, as well. 'Yeesh! I said keep your voice down, man. Look, you want to find out about Medici, all you need to do is read a few back issues. But don't do it here. Get away from the paper, go to the library, someplace anonymous.'

Anonymous? 'Last time I checked, this was a national newspaper, Harry. One of the major players. When did we start letting the creeps run the show?'

Harry rolled his chair across the cubicle and out the door. He looked almost surprised to find nobody eavesdropping and shrugged as he scooted back to his desk. Watching, Gren tried to ignore the slowly tightening knot in his stomach.

'Nobody's running the show, okay? I'm just saying you'll have competition on this one, and you might be putting more than your career on the line. But, hey, you wanna stick your neck out, go right ahead. Just don't expect me to put mine on the block beside you. I do research, that's all. I'm not looking for headlines, and I don't have a death wish.' His voice fell to a whisper once again. 'You'll find out, but be careful. Medici's not real fond of reporters these days.'

Harry grabbed a manilla folder from the stack on the corner of his desk, flipped it open, and began to read. In other words, thought Gren, time's up. 'You've been a big help,' he said, carefully pocketing the disk as he turned to walk away.

'Don't mention it.'

Harry's tone of voice left no room for doubt. He meant precisely what he'd said — *don't mention it*. The knot in Gren's stomach twisted again. Frank Medici, whoever he was, had the usually cool and logical Harry May thoroughly spooked. If Medici was this scary, no wonder Nikki was afraid to talk about her past.

Suddenly, Gren felt the need to move quickly. He hurried to the elevator at the end of the hall and jabbed the call button, pacing impatiently back-and-forth as he waited. Harry was right. He'd be better off using the archives at the public library. Not that he cared if some staff reporter caught wind of a new Medici story, but if Medici himself caught on . . . He had no intention of laying down a trail that might lead the man to Nikki and Claire.

Gren bounded onto the elevator the moment the doors slid open. Reality struck before they had time to close again. He'd already left a trail. Last week. Three days of searches on every missing child database in the country. How many times had he keyed in detailed descriptions of Nikki and Claire? Countless times. More than enough to attract Frank Medici's attention. More than enough to point a finger at Vinegar Hill.

★   ★   ★

A cool breeze ruffled the curtains and with it, from beyond the hedgerow of dogwood and willow, came the faint but growing sound of a car approaching from the west, a sound that always reminded Nikki of wind in a tunnel. She waited, listening. Instead of blowing past and fading away, this car seemed to be slowing down. Gren?

The thought of seeing him again sent her heart racing, a warm thrill of anticipation coursing through her veins. And then a moment's apprehension.

She smoothed the front of her T-shirt, ran her fingers through her hair, wishing she had time to run upstairs and change. *No way!* What on earth was the matter with her? She drew a deep breath and let it out, slowly. Better. Well, sort of. She straightened her shirt again. Nervous or not, she was going to tell him everything. Right away, before the jitters got the best of her. How hard could it be? She'd practiced the words at least a dozen times, and that was just today. Gren would understand what she'd had to do and why she'd kept it secret. She was certain of that now. He'd understand and he would help.

Nikki looked out the window again, just in time to watch a car round the bend — not Gren's red Mustang after all, but a dusty, dented sedan, gunmetal gray. It rolled to a halt at the edge of the yard.

In the space of a single heartbeat, her nervous anticipation vanished, swept away in a mind-numbing rush of fear. She could see two people inside the car — dark, shadowy figures. For a long moment neither of them moved, then the driver's door swung slowly open.

Tearing her gaze away from the window, Nikki shot an anxious glance at Claire. Blissfully unaware of the approaching strangers, the baby smiled a sleepy smile, snuggling Raggedy Man against her cheek. It seemed so normal, so safe. Was she doing it again? Jumping to all the wrong conclusions? Turning back to the window, she felt her heart leap. The dark-suited man emerging from the car looked anything but normal and safe. Eyes hidden behind a pair of mirrored sunglasses, lips frozen in a tight, grim line, he looked angry — and dangerous.

The wind caught at his jacket as he rounded the front of the car, giving Nikki a glimpse of the shoulder holster and gun hidden beneath. She knew she should run, grab Claire and escape before it was too late, but her feet seemed to be stuck fast to the floor. Steadying herself against the counter, she watched, eyes wide with fright, as the passenger door swung open and the second stranger stepped out of the car. But not a stranger . . .

No! This couldn't be real! If not for her death-grip on the edge of the counter, Nikki would have hit the floor when her knees buckled under her. 'Lainey . . . ' The word was little more than a dry whisper. She gasped for air — short, shallow breaths — too much, too fast. Spots swam before her eyes, blood roared in her ears, and every second she delayed brought Lainey and her dangerous-looking companion one step closer to the house.

It's all up to you now.

She pushed herself away from the window, forced her legs to carry her across the room. It couldn't be Lainey. Lainey was dead. With her gaze locked on the screen door, she pulled Claire and Raggedy Man out of the highchair and backed through the doorway to Gren's private wing, ready to run. As she turned, the breeze blew again, carrying a scrap of conversation her way.

'*Get what we came for.*'

Nikki stumbled, leaned heavily against the wall, her senses reeling. She knew that voice as well as she knew her own. Lainey was back from the dead.

14

The screen door shrieked a warning. They were in the house, maybe right behind her. Lainey's grim companion could be pointing that gun of his at her back, even now. Would she hear the shot? Or would the pain come first? And afterwards . . . dear God, what would happen to Claire?

Run! Down the hall, through Gren's bedroom, and out into the rose garden. Footsteps echoed behind her, not ghostly, but real. People didn't come back from the dead. No, Lainey and her thug were very much alive, determined to 'get what they came for'. But what? The money? The disk? Claire? *No!*

She sprinted across the lawn, tension knotting every muscle, anticipating the blast, the searing impact of bullet into flesh. *Why?* Why had Lainey abandoned her child, let her own sister

275

believe the worst for all these months? Had she planned the whole thing — some sort of elaborate scam? Nikki didn't even want to think it, much less let herself believe it, but what other explanation could there be? How incredibly stupid of Lainey — and typically reckless. Did she honestly think she could steal from a man like Frank Medici and get away with it?

Keep moving! She looked back. Had they seen her? *Don't stop!* This had to be a nightmare, a slow motion run going nowhere. She hung onto that flicker of hope for a brief moment longer, tried to believe it was just a bad dream, another mindbending fever. She'd awaken in a moment and find herself in Gren's arms, his lips cool against her cheek, his voice gentle and reassuring. But her body knew the truth. Her feet felt like lead, the baby in her arms an impossible weight. *Run!* This was one nightmare that wouldn't end if she fell.

Another few steps and she and Claire

would disappear into the cornfield. She could see the red tile roof and broad, square chimneys of Ravensleigh in the distance. With Gren away, Noble Bateman was her best, her only hope. Heart pounding, she dove at the green wall of corn, pushed her way through, and forced herself to keep running. Claire screamed.

'Shhhh . . . shhhh. Honey, be quiet, please . . . ' She couldn't say more. Already her lungs were on fire, each sharp breath a new blast of heat and flame. Pressing the baby's head against her chest, she tried to shield the child with her own body. Leaves whipped across her face and arms, sharp-edged and cruel. Fallen stalks and roots and clods of earth sprang up to trip her. By some miracle, she stayed on her feet, praying for the strength to go on.

From the nursery window, the field had always looked so beautiful — straight rows of lush, green leaves and golden tassels. But here on the ground, those rows disappeared. Wind rattled the corn stalks and shivered through the leaves. She felt so lost, with nothing to mark her place or guide her way, just an angry sea of green, and above her, dark and threatening, the loveless gray sky.

Were they following? She couldn't tell. Beyond the awful, relentless pounding of her own heart, Claire's frantic wail was the only sound she could hear. *Don't look back!* Don't think about them. Just keep running, one foot in front of the other.

Nikki swiped at a trickle of moisture on her face — blood! But how — Had he pulled the trigger after all? *Don't think it! Keep running, don't stop!* They might be right behind.

Without warning, the green corn jungle gave way to open lawn. Ravensleigh! She stumbled across the grass, followed the flagstone path to the end of the garden and the white frame handyman's cottage. No one followed. Claire would be safe now, if she could just find Noble. Only a few more steps to the door . . .

It flew open before she had a chance to knock. Good thing, because she wasn't at all certain she could have lifted her arm.

'Saints preserve us, little Missy, what's happened to you?'

Lifting the still-sobbing Claire from her arms, Noble led the way to the kitchen. 'Sit yourself down at the table, now, and tell me what's wrong.'

It took Nikki a long moment to catch her breath and find her voice. 'C-Claire . . . is . . . is she all right?'

The baby had stopped crying. Resting her head on Noble's broad chest, she tucked her thumb into her mouth and stared across the room at Nikki — wide, dark eyes in a tear-streaked face.

'Madder than a wet hen a second ago. More tired than anythin' now, I suspect.'

'There was b-blood.'

Noble looked down at the child, gently running his hands through her hair and along her arms. 'Not hers, little Missy. Just a few scratches.' He nodded in Nikki's direction. 'You got yourself corn slashed, didn't you? What on earth were you doin' out in that field? Were you lost?'

'I w-wanted to be . . . ' The words faded out in a sob. *Don't cry!* She swiped impatiently at her watering eyes. If she lost control now, she'd never be able to do what had to be done. Her face felt hot and puffy, the tears stung as they trickled down her cheeks. Corn slashed? She looked down at her arms. Sure enough, they were covered with long, red welts from the razor-sharp leaves. Some of the scratches were bleeding, all of them had begun to burn and itch. She could feel the painful welts rising on her face and neck, too, and sobbed again, in spite of herself.

'I'll get you some water,' said Noble quietly. 'Just let me put the wee one down. Plumb tuckered out, she is.'

Nikki watched as he pulled open the curtain at the end of the room. Behind it was a small alcove, space enough for a bed and dresser, but not much more. With loving care, Noble settled Claire in the center of the bed, covered her with a quilt, and kissed her forehead.

'She'll be just fine, Missy. Now, let's get you cleaned up.'

'No.' She pushed to her feet and tottered across the room to stand in front of him, ignoring his startled expression. 'I don't have time, Noble. I need you to listen to me, and trust me, and try to understand. Can you do that?'

He nodded, gently touching her arm. 'But won't you sit for a bit? Have some tea, maybe? It'd make you feel better . . . '

'No time. Claire's in danger, Noble. That's why we were running through the field.'

'Danger? From what . . . who — ' His face blanched. 'You're not sayin' that Gren — '

'No! Gren's not even home. It's my . . . m-my . . . ' Another sob rose in her throat. This time she let it out, let the tears fall, too. It would've been pointless to try to stop them.

Noble stepped close, wrapping her safe in his arms, holding tight. Oh, how she wished they were Gren's arms.

'You can tell me, Missy. It'll be all right.'

She longed to believe him. But Noble couldn't make things right. Only she could do that. And Lainey.

'My s-sister,' she said at last. 'I thought she was dead, b-but she's here, at Wilder House. She's in some kind of trouble, Noble. And we have to keep Claire out of it.'

'Trouble?' He stepped back, holding her at arms' length to study her face. 'What trouble?'

'That's what I'm going to find out. Promise me you'll keep Claire safe. *Promise.*'

'You know I will, Missy, but — '

'No. No buts. I have to do this by myself, and I have to know that nothing will happen to Claire. Promise you won't let anyone hurt her, or take her . . . no matter what?'

He nodded. 'No matter what.'

It was Nikki's turn, now, to study him. What was he thinking, she wondered? Would he try to follow her or send the police? 'One more promise, okay?'

He didn't answer, just lifted one bushy eyebrow and waited.

'I'll explain everything once I've talked to my sister. That's *my* promise, Noble. But I need to be sure you won't try to interfere. Stay here until I call you. And no police, okay?'

He made a helpless little shrug. 'I said I'd trust you, Missy, and I will. But how long — '

'Soon, Noble. This won't take a lot of time.' Turning, she limped toward the door, her ankles stiff and throbbing. She'd twisted them more than once on the long run through the field.

'Missy?'

She looked over her shoulder.

283

'Take the station wagon. The keys are by the door.'

★　★　★

Be logical, stay focused — *one fact, one piece of the puzzle at a time.*

Gren's hands tightened on the steering wheel, a nervous, convulsive grip that didn't feel logical at all. He'd made the trip home from Toronto in record time, forty minutes to think about exactly what he'd done, about how to *undo* it before Nikki and Claire had to pay the price. He'd almost managed to convince himself he hadn't dug deeply enough to attract Frank Medici's attention. Faint hope, but better than the fear he'd been fighting since Harry issued his dire warning. Faint hope had flown out the window two seconds ago.

He considered the cause, a battered, gray car left blocking the driveway, both front doors standing open. The too-familiar knot in his stomach twisted painfully once more.

Don't leap to conclusions. After nearly eight months in Vinegar Hill, Nikki would know people, friends or customers who might visit.

Not a customer. Not driving that car. Pulling the key from the ignition, Gren pushed the Mustang's door open and stepped out onto the gravel laneway. He stared up at the afternoon sky, dark and heavy with rain clouds, and wished for some sunshine to warm his face, maybe chase the chill of apprehension shivering through him. Every instinct told him to run, get to the house, find Nikki.

Instead he moved cautiously past the gray car, pausing long enough to make a quick check of the interior, leaning inside to feel behind the visors and under the front seat. Nothing. But the driver wasn't local. A map, open on the dashboard, confirmed it. And perched beside the map, two cans of cola, fizzing softly. *Not local and not alone.*

Gren stared grimly at the collection

of empty coffee cups and fast food bags littering the back seat. Noble always said you could tell a lot about a person by the state of the car they drove. *Right again, old man.* But how long had they been on the road? How long had they been searching?

Drawing a deep, silent breath, Gren tried once again to focus his thoughts, to keep his mind from racing off in a dozen terrifying directions as he bolted across the driveway and into the yard. He lost the battle when he stooped to pick Claire's Raggedy Man out of the dirt. The sprout would not go quietly without her doll. Was he too late?

Please, let them be safe.

He ran, taking cover in the willow hedgerow, sprinting across the lawn and through the rose garden, stopping short on the patio at the door to his bedroom. It stood open. Not all the way, just far enough for someone to slip out . . . or in.

The house was too quiet. He crossed the bedroom, stood listening at the door.

If Nikki had friends in the kitchen, there would be voices, laughter. *Face it! She's in trouble.* He dropped the rag doll onto the bed, tried not to look at the sad, dirty face that reminded him so much of Claire. Easing the door open, he chanced one quick step into the hall, long enough to glimpse the stranger seated at the kitchen table, back to the door, suit jacket slung carelessly over a chair. Long enough for the threatening image of a black leather shoulder holster to burn itself into his mind.

Gren ducked back into the bedroom, enduring a moment of terror, of cold, grasping fingers closing tight around his heart. He fought the painfully familiar sensation. Had he lost another love, another family? The thought of it was more than he could bear. *Do something!* But what?

Slipping into the silent hallway again, he edged toward the open kitchen door, hugging the wall, careful to avoid each creaky board in the old hardwood floor.

Don't turn around. Don't turn around. The words ran over and over in his mind, as if by sheer force of will he could keep the stranger seated and unsuspecting, keep him focused on that copy of the Vinegar Hill Economist spread before him on the table. Gren hesitated in the doorway, holding his breath, certain the man would hear the terrible pounding of his heart, the rush of blood in his ears. No sign of Nikki. No sign of the stranger's cola-drinking partner, either. What if . . .

He fought the dark thoughts that flooded his mind, thoughts of what Nikki might be enduring, right now, at the hands of the second intruder. Pushing through his fear, he scanned the room. He needed a weapon, something . . . *anything* . . . His gaze settled on the cast iron skillet. Not the best plan he'd ever come up with but, hell, it had worked once before, right here in this very room.

The stranger yawned, stretched, shifted restlessly in his seat. For one awful moment Gren was certain he was about to stand up. Instead he rattled the newspaper, flipped to the center, and smoothed it out on the table again, intent on some titbit of local news. Gren took advantage of the moment, moving swiftly across the kitchen, three long, silent strides. He had the skillet in his hand before the paper stopped rustling. This was almost too easy . . . and it just might work. He took up the mantra again as he maneuvered closer. *Don't turn around. Don't turn around. Don't . . .*

Too late, Gren saw the gun. Not safely holstered, but poised on the kitchen table, a hair's breadth away from the stranger's right hand.

Scratch 'easy'. He raised his arms, holding the skillet in a two-fisted grip. *Get it right the first time, Wilder, 'cause you won't have a second chance.*

'No!'

Nikki? The skillet arced downward, gaining momentum. Should he pull back?

289

'Murphy! *Look out!*'

The voice, from just beyond the kitchen door, was like Nikki's . . . but different, somehow. And the shriek of warning brought the stranger to his feet. As he rose, Gren landed a glancing blow to the side of his head, but the man never faltered, turning to face him, grim and murderously alert.

'*Freeze!*'

He froze, staring down the barrel of a revolver pointed squarely between his eyes. Murphy's finger twitched on the trigger, his cold gray gaze locked on target. *No second chance.* Gren's throat tightened painfully. Wasn't this the part where his life was supposed to flash before his eyes? Well to hell with that. If this *was* the end, he wanted to see Nikki one last time, look into her eyes and know the truth. Was that really her voice he'd heard? Had she intended the warning for Murphy or for him?

Tearing his gaze away from the gun and the scowling man who held it,

290

Gren scanned the room. Where was she?

'Put the damned frying pan down,' snarled Murphy, taking a single step back and gesturing toward the table. He lowered his aim to somewhere around Gren's heart.

'Sure.' He let the skillet fall from his hand, putting just enough of a spin on the heavy pan to send it careening toward Murphy's feet.

The man sidestepped and spat an obscenity, but his aim didn't waver. 'Not too smart, Wilder.'

What the hell . . . *He knows my name!* Gren wrestled for another brief moment with the possibility that Nikki hadn't been hiding out at Wilder House at all, but laying low, waiting for her lover, her partner in crime, to show up. Had she played him for the fool, let him fall for a memory, a ghost of all that was good about his life, all that was gone forever?

Please, Gren . . . don't let them hurt Claire.

No. No way. He couldn't have been so wrong about her. He'd seen the fear, the terror in Nikki's eyes. And more than that, he'd seen the beginnings of trust. She'd depended on him . . . was still depending on him. And so was Claire. He knew it now as surely as he knew he'd give his life for them.

Meeting Murphy's steely gaze once more, Gren drew a deep breath and took a chance. 'Nikki? Where are you?'

'That's what we'd like to know,' muttered Murphy. 'Sit down, will you? And shut up.' Waving Gren into the chair he'd just vacated, Murphy lifted one hand to his temple and moaned. Apparently his brush with the skillet hadn't gone unnoticed after all.

Gren bit back a smile of satisfaction as he sank onto the chair. 'Headache, Murphy?'

'I said, *shut up*.' Murphy moved to the end of the table, back to the wall this time, and straddled a chair, all without shifting his gaze or his aim away from Gren.

'Murph? You okay?'

That voice again, so familiar but not quite right.

Murphy growled an answer. 'Yeah. You can come out now.'

Gren swivelled in his chair, catching his breath at first sight of the woman who sounded so like Nikki. Not even close. This was no elfin wisp of a girl. Emerging from the shadows of the stairwell, she moved slowly across the room, her long, graceful legs sheathed in clingy, leopard-print tights. Crouching beside Murphy's chair, she rested one hand on his arm, lifting the other to trace the new swelling on his temple with her fingertips.

'Poor Murph,' she said softly, then flashed a scathing glance in Gren's direction. 'Why'd you do that?'

'Forget it,' said Murphy, brushing her hand away. 'Just tell him what we need and let's get out of here.'

The woman straightened abruptly, planting her hands on her hips, a gesture that pulled the faded ochre fabric of her shirt taut across ample breasts and a tiny waist. 'We had a deal, Murphy. Don't you *dare* try to weasel out on me now. Not until . . . '

Her voice trailed off. Gren tried to read the look that passed between Murphy and the woman. Her voice sounded angry, accusing, but her eyes held only desperation. *Take advantage of the moment.*

'I know what you want.' Blunt and to the point. Effective, too. In the space of a heartbeat he had their complete and undivided attention. 'Listen carefully, because I'm only going to say this once.'

The woman curled herself onto the chair opposite his, propped her elbows on the table, and rested her chin in her hands, watching him and waiting.

Murphy studied him for a long moment, then laid the gun on the table and folded his arms across his chest. 'So . . . spit it out, Wilder. What do we want?'

Gren let the silence ripen a bit

before he answered.

'Money.' Would they buy his bluff? 'And information.' Or would they realize he was making it up on the fly? 'A certain computer disk I'd imagine you're quite anxious to retrieve.'

Murphy moved his right hand back to the table, nudging the gun with his thumb. 'Go on.'

'And you think you want Nikki. But you don't.'

'We don't?' Murphy met his gaze and held it.

'Murph? Shouldn't we — '

Gren wasn't sure how Murphy managed to silence the woman with only a glance, but he wasn't about to waste time figuring it out. 'No,' he continued. 'You don't. As a matter of fact, she's the least of your worries right now.'

'Is that so?' Murphy's gaze slid down to the gun on the table. 'And I suppose you're going to tell us what we *should* be worried about?'

Right. Just as soon as I figure it out

myself. Gren tried to swallow the lump in his throat. It wouldn't go away. 'I finished a story this morning. Interesting stuff about numbers and names. One name in particular.'

'Murph?' There was no mistaking the panic in the woman's voice. She grabbed Murphy's sleeve with both hands.

'Look, Wilder, you've got it all wrong.'

'I don't think so,' Gren interrupted. 'I think I've got it exactly right. I think you're going to take your money and your disk and walk away from this. *Now.* Because if anything happens to me, or to — '

A flicker of motion beyond the screen door caught his attention, set his heart rate soaring. He gulped a deep breath, suddenly unable to remember what he should say next, watching helplessly as a slight figure in blue jeans and a white T-shirt darted across the lawn. *Nikki! No, not now!*

Desperate to warn her, Gren sprang

to his feet, letting the chair clatter across the tile floor behind him.

'Hey!' Murphy was on his feet in an instant, leveling the gun.

Gren forced himself to look away from the door. He had to buy Nikki some time, warn her, protect her. Meeting Murphy's gaze with what he hoped was an arrogant sneer, he raised his voice and played his trump card. 'Nobody's seen the story yet, Murphy. Make the right choice and nobody ever will. But know this. I made a copy of your disk. Kill me and it goes straight to the cops. What do you think Frank Medici will do to you and your girlfriend then?'

The woman gave an audible gasp and buried her face in her hands. Murphy winced. 'Like I said, Wilder, you've got it all wrong. Now sit, before somebody gets hurt.'

From the doorway, a calm, determined voice answered, 'Put the gun down. *Nobody's* going to get hurt.'

15

'It's here. Your money and your disk. That's what you came for . . . right?'

Nikki's hand trembled as she pushed open the screen door, body and soul as shaky as a leaf in the wind. But she couldn't give in. If she let the fear win, she might as well let them win, too, and that wasn't part of the plan. Lainey could have her money, and her precious disk, but she would not take Claire. Not to be part of a life on the run, bought and paid for with stolen money.

She met Gren's gaze across the room, saw the fear etched on his face — not for himself, but for her. If only she'd told him the truth when she'd had the chance. How would he ever forgive her deception?

Dragging the heavy gym bag behind her, Nikki limped through the door and across the kitchen. Pure adrenaline had brought her this far, given her the strength to haul Lainey's 'insurance' out of the garden shed and across the lawn, the nerve to seek a confrontation. But now, uncertain of what to do next, she felt all that chemical courage fading away.

'Cat?'

A voice from the grave. Slowly, Nikki straightened, turning to face her sister, avoiding Gren's steady gaze. She couldn't bear to watch him react to the news that even her name was a lie.

'Oh, Cat . . . ' Lainey moved quickly toward her, arms outstretched. 'What on earth happened to you?'

Nikki tried to back away but her feet wouldn't move. Helpless, she stared at Lainey, then at the tall, white-shirted man at the end of the table. Her gaze locked on the gun in his right hand. A gun that was pointed directly at Gren. She stumbled, knocking over a chair.

'What happened?' repeated Lainey, catching her by the arm. 'You look like hell.'

Across the room the man's hand began to move. Nikki watched his aim slide away from Gren. Maybe he'd decided on a new target. *Yes! Shoot me, not him. Please . . . not Gren.* She clenched her fists, willing herself to be brave — or at least to *look* brave.

'Cat, where's my — '

'No!' *Don't ask. Please, don't ask about Claire, not yet. I can't let Gren find out this way.* 'I . . . I thought you were d-dead.' *Just like I'm going to be in a minute.* Nikki drew a deep breath and held it, certain it was her last. The gun was still moving, slow and steady . . . or maybe she was seeing in slow motion. Her world, her personal hell on earth, seemed to have slowed to a painful crawl.

She didn't dare look at Gren. It was bad enough imagining the hurt and betrayal she'd find in his eyes. She could only pray he wouldn't try anything stupid like tackling the man or lunging for the gun. Now was not the time to be a hero. *One of us has to stay alive . . . for Claire.*

'Dead,' said Lainey quietly. 'I know. And I'm so sorry, Cat.'

'*Sorry?*' She caught the edge of the table and held on. To hell with dying bravely, standing on her own two feet. If the creep was going to shoot her, he could shoot her sitting down.

As her knees buckled, she felt Lainey's arm around her waist, easing her gently onto a chair. Across the room, her companion slipped his gun into its holster. Nikki waited until he'd snapped the leather restraint into place before letting out a pent-up breath. She met Lainey's gaze. 'Sorry's not enough. Not after everything you put us through. How *could* you?'

'Cat, please . . . I can explain.'

'Yeah, you were always good at coming up with an explanation when you had to. Well, maybe I don't want to hear it, Lainey. Maybe I — '

From the corner of her eye Nikki saw the white-shirted man reach for his jacket, draped over the back of a nearby chair. His movements were careful, deliberate, as if he had every right to be in her kitchen, as if she and Gren were the intruders in Wilder House. She watched nervously as he searched one pocket, then another. What was he looking for? A bigger gun?

'He's a cop,' said Lainey, as if reading her mind.

Right on cue, the man produced a badge and photo ID from the depths of his jacket pocket, tossing them onto the table. 'Murphy,' he said simply. A shrug was his only response to Gren's muttered outrage.

'Sergeant Murphy,' said Lainey, after a brief, awkward silence. 'R.C.M.P.'

A cop? Nikki looked at the man again, recalling the two Vancouver detectives who'd been so eager to hand her over to Frank Medici. Why should this one be any different? 'So, he's a cop. Is that supposed to make me feel better?'

Lainey shrugged. 'Hopefully. Once you've heard the whole story.' Glancing over her shoulder she added, 'Sit down, will you, Murph? You're making me nervous.'

'*I'm* making *you* nervous? Good one.' For a moment, Murphy looked as if he might actually smile. Instead he winced and touched the side of his head. 'Okay with you if I get some ice, maybe a couple of aspirin?'

'Good plan.' Lainey waved him away. 'Poor Murph. Your boyfriend walloped him but good.'

'My boy — ' Nikki glanced across the table at Gren. He'd been studying Murphy's ID but looked up to meet her gaze.

'Frying pan,' he said dryly. 'Seemed like a good idea at the time.'

'Lucky for me,' said Murphy, 'he's not a very good shot. Now, about that aspirin?'

'Over the s-sink,' stammered Nikki, hating the tremor in her voice, wishing she could have been there to see Gren wield the skillet. Too bad it hadn't worked.

Focusing on her sister's face once again, she wrapped her arms around herself and held on, determined to keep Lainey from seeing how badly her hands were shaking. 'So explain. Explain how you've managed to be dead for nine months but now you're alive. Explain why you left — '

'Cat, I don't have a lot of time.' Lainey righted the fallen chair and sat perched on the edge of the seat. 'Give me a chance, okay?'

Wasn't that how it always went? Lainey screwed up, Lainey begged for another chance. Nikki sighed. 'I'm listening.'

'First . . . where's my baby?'

Oh, no . . .

Gren's reaction to the inevitable question tugged mightily at Nikki's conscience — his sharp intake of breath, the dull 'thunk' as Murphy's badge fell from his fingers onto the polished pine table. *Don't judge me yet. Just listen. Listen and understand.*

'*Your* baby?'

304

'Cat . . .'

'No. Not Cat. I stopped being Catherine Salter nearly nine months ago, because of you. *Explain that.* Then we'll talk about Claire.'

'Claire? Is that what you call her now?' Lainey's hopeful smile vanished as the silence grew. 'I . . . it was the only way.'

'To do what?' demanded Nikki. 'Steal Frank Medici's money?'

Her sister's already pale face lost every hint of color. Tears brimmed in her eyes, trickling slowly down her cheeks as she nervously twisted a strand of hair around her finger — one habit the two of them had always shared.

What was it about her that seemed so different? It wasn't until Lainey lifted her left hand to brush the tears away that Nikki figured it out. Her fingers were bare — no clusters of diamonds, no carefully enameled nails. The elegant, picture-perfect makeup was missing, too. Even her thick, black hair seemed to have lost its shine, hanging limply around her shoulders.

'That money's mine,' she said softly, 'not Frank's. I earned it, Cat. At the club, back in Calgary. Every penny. And now it's my — Now it belongs to Claire.' She swiped at the tears again, sniffing loudly before she continued.

'You were right about Frank. I should've listened but I didn't want to believe. By the time I figured it out . . .

'Cat, I ran away nearly two months before the baby came. Frank doesn't even know she's alive.' She stared at Murphy for a long moment, as if wishing she could find a way to blame it all on him, then slowly shook her head. 'They said I should give her up, let some nice family adopt her . . . '

Lainey accepted a handful of tissue from Murphy but didn't bother to dry her face. 'I just couldn't do it. We're her family, Cat. And I . . . I knew you'd love her for me.'

Not for you. 'You still haven't said why.'

'To put Frank away.'

'What? But how — '

'I went back, said I'd lost the baby — y'know, a miscarriage. Then I said how much I loved him and needed him, convinced him we were meant for each other, played the perfect wife. It was — ' Lainey shuddered, twisting the handful of tissue in her lap, uttering a low, tortured groan.

'Murphy's people told me what to look for. It's taken me all this time to gather the bits and pieces, Cat, but it's done. We have the evidence that's going to put Frank away forever.'

Forever? Was it possible? Was Lainey doing the right thing, taking a stand for the first time in her life? If so, she'd made a very dangerous choice and a very dangerous enemy in Frank Medici.

'I know what you're thinking,' said Lainey, squaring her shoulders and smiling weakly. 'But don't worry. I'm not going to end up like those other witnesses. Murphy here promised. And, in case you haven't figured it out already, I trust him.' She drew a deep

307

breath. 'Only trouble is, once it's all over I have to disappear. No more Lainey.'

'No more . . . ' *Get what we came for.* Of course! That's what this was all about. She was planning a new life — life after Frank — and she meant to take Claire.

Unable to resist the waves of sorrow washing over her, Nikki moaned . . . a soft, keening sound she prayed no one else would hear. How could she stand to lose the baby she'd loved for all these months? Her family. But not her child. What right did she have to try to keep Claire from her mother?

Gren's fingers touched the back of her hand, an unspoken promise, her life line in the storm. Nikki grabbed on and held tight, overwhelmed by the sudden realization that, despite everything, he was still on her side, still ready to help. But she could sense his pain, too, as real and as deep as her own. What would this do to him? Would he survive the loss of another beloved child?

Feeling helpless, unable to speak, she waited for her sister to continue.

Lainey's breath shuddered out on a sigh. 'But I couldn't. I said I *wouldn't* go without telling you the truth, without seeing my baby one last time.'

'L-last time?' Nikki struggled to catch her breath. What a strange feeling, as if her heart had suddenly started beating again. Gren held her hand a little tighter.

'Please, Cat, I know it's a lot to ask, but I *can't* take her with me. I'd never be absolutely certain she was safe. You do understand, don't you? Cat?'

Understand?

'Oh boy,' grumbled Murphy, sinking back onto his chair at the end of the table. 'Here we go again.'

'Don't cry, Cat . . . '

She wasn't crying, was she?

'It'll be all right, I promise.' Lainey reached for her, pulling her close. 'Come here. Give your big sister a hug.'

A hug? She simply couldn't do it. What if Lainey's story changed again?

Clinging to Gren's hand, she stammered the only truth that mattered anymore. 'I l-love her, Lainey.'

'Well, of course you do. How could you help it?'

'I thought you were d-dead. And then . . . then I thought . . . '

'You thought exactly what we wanted you to think. And for Claire's sake, you have to keep right on believing it. Your sister is dead.'

'I hate to break this up,' said Murphy, 'but we're running out of time here.'

Lainey pulled away, pressing a knot of twisted tissue into Nikki's free hand. She fired a dirty look at the Mountie. 'Stick to business, eh, Murph? Well you'd better remember our deal — first I see my daughter, then we go.'

He nodded, 'I haven't forgotten, but — '

'No! No buts. You promised. Just a little time, that's all I asked. And you *promised*.'

'Yes, I did.' He reached across the table as he spoke, resting his hand on

Lainey's shoulder, giving a gentle squeeze. 'I also promised to keep you alive.'

'But don't you see? This is why staying alive was so important, Murph. One last chance to make things right with the people who really count.' Lainey shrugged, taking his hand between hers. 'And anyway, Frank doesn't suspect. There's no way. You said so yourself.'

No way? 'Oh, God. Lainey, I . . . I went to the police but they . . . I think they were working for Frank.'

Nikki began to tremble again. What if she'd ruined everything? What if, because of her, Frank Medici knew all about the carefully laid plans to put him in jail?

Suddenly desperate to return her sister's 'insurance', she tried to pull free of Gren's gentle grasp. For a brief moment, he resisted, tightening his hold on her hand, forcing her to look up, to meet his gaze. Worry deepened the lines on his forehead and darkened his eyes. He had something to say, but what? Did he doubt Lainey's story? Or was he only now realizing the depth and breadth of the lie they'd been living?

Whatever his concerns, Gren kept them to himself, letting his gaze slide back to the tabletop as he freed her hand. She'd never felt more alone. *Don't give up on us . . . not yet.*

Pushing stiffly away from the table, Nikki dropped to her knees beside the musty gym bag. A sudden wash of tears blurred her vision, left her fumbling with the rusty zipper. Why wouldn't her fingers obey?

'Yeah,' said Lainey, sounding strangely calm. 'You went to the cops. The mystery woman. Don't worry. Murphy covered for you.'

Murphy? Nikki wiped her eyes with the back of her hand. 'I showed them a picture . . . '

'But you didn't tell them your name. Or mine. Smart.' Lainey flashed a proud smile. '*Smart.*'

Not smart — lucky. 'I didn't have a chance. They made the connection themselves when they saw that old picture. They said there was a body. S-said it might be you, wanted me to identify . . . '

Her throat tightened, cutting off the words. Even now, with Lainey close enough to touch, she couldn't shake the image that had haunted her for so long — dark water and lifeless eyes. Never more than her own imagination, but it still felt so real.

'Cat? You all right?'

When Lainey's fingers brushed against her cheek, warm and very much alive, the image vanished. With it went any lingering doubts she might have had about her sister's intentions. 'I'm fine.'

Grabbing the zipper, Nikki tugged with all her might. It wouldn't budge. She felt so weak, so useless, so *stupid*. She'd been ready to trust those Vancouver detectives, ready to tell them everything. What would've happened to

Lainey then? What would've happened to Claire? 'I overheard them talking. They said something about Frank, and — '

Lainey interrupted with a bitter laugh. 'Frank was steamed about that. Hey, take it easy, will you?' She knelt, gently brushing Nikki's hands away, and jimmied the stubborn zipper. It stuck once, then gave way with a gnash of teeth.

'Picture it. Frank Medici gets called down to the morgue to look at some stranger, then finds out somebody else has been asking questions, flashing a picture that looks a lot like his missing wife.' She winked. 'Funny how that snapshot disappeared, eh, sis? I'm surprised those cops are still walking around. Murph says we'll get them, too, before it's all over.'

'You mean they don't have the picture? But how — Murphy?'

'One of his team.' Lainey fished the disk case out of the bag and passed it to Murphy. 'Listen, Cat, I know what you must be thinking — that we used you and the baby, put you in all kinds of danger. But you need to know . . . you were never alone back there in Gastown.'

'Never — What do you mean?'

'You had protection, right from the start. Your friend Garth, for instance . . . '

'Garth? But he's — '

'An ex-con?' Lainey grinned. 'Can you think of a better cover for a cop?' She sprang to her feet, pulling Nikki along with her. Giving the gym bag a kick, she added, 'Might want to put that in the bank. Our little girl deserves a college fund, don't you think?'

Our little girl. 'Are you sure about all this, Lainey? *Really* sure?'

Lainey didn't answer right away, just reached for her hand and held on tight. 'Yes,' she said at last, 'I'm sure. Scared witless, but sure. Want to know what I ask myself, whenever I start feeling really panicked? *'What would Cat do?'* Keeps me on the right track, y'know?'

'That's not what I meant.'

'I know what you meant. And that's the one thing I don't have doubts about — ever. Claire belongs here with you, safe and happy. You're the only mother she's ever known. Now, come on, will you? Let's go see her.'

'We're not going anywhere,' said Murphy, turning a stone cold gaze on Gren. He tossed the plastic case, open and empty, onto the table. 'Where the hell is the disk, Wilder? This isn't a story, y'know. Not your story, anyway.'

Gren stared at the empty case, tension knotting his shoulders and throbbing behind his eyes. Was that what Nikki thought, too? That he'd be willing to risk their lives for a story? *Damn*. He'd dug himself a deep hole this time. And the light at the top was quickly receding.

Why the hell had he taken the disk in the first place, instead of staying, facing her with his questions? More importantly, why hadn't he handed it off to Murphy the minute Nikki reached for that old gym bag? The answer was almost painfully simple. Giving it back meant proving her right. She never should have trusted him.

'*Gren?*'

Only one word, but the apprehension in her voice said it all. *How could you do this to us?* Suddenly the disk in his breast pocket felt cold, weighing heavy against his heart, a burden of guilt he couldn't wait to unload.

He stood, tossing the disk to Murphy as he rounded the table. Catching Nikki's hand in his, he pulled her close, sheltering her in his arms. Somehow, he had to make her understand. It might have started as a quest for the story but, in the end, all he'd wanted was to understand her fear.

'Nikki, I — '

Murphy interrupted. 'Hand over the copy, too, Wilder. Or should I say copies? And then try to convince me we can count on you to keep quiet. That disk makes our case, connects Frank to the evidence. Like I said, this isn't *your* story. It can't be.'

Cursing the man for doing his job, Gren tightened his hold on Nikki. She didn't resist, slumping against him as if the effort of staying on her feet was suddenly too much for her.

'There are no copies.' He spoke softly, pressing his lips against her hair. What Lainey and her Mountie chose to believe didn't concern him. The only person who mattered now was sobbing in his arms. 'No story, either. It was never about a story. *Never*. Nikki, it was about you, about us. And Claire. I only wanted to help.'

Little by little her arms twined around his waist, until Nikki was holding him just as tightly as he held her . . . as if their very lives depended on it.

Relief spilled over him in a torrent. She was giving him a second chance. A chance to prove he'd learned from the past. Releasing a breath he hadn't been conscious of holding, Gren met the Mountie's gaze once more.

'Medici's not the only name on the list, Murphy. You're going after all of them, right?'

Murphy shook his head. 'Straw men, Wilder. That's all they are. Frank's little imaginary empire.'

'Straw men?'

'That's right. Not one of them really exists.' Murphy gave a wry smile as he pocketed the disk. 'All those numbered corporations are doing a fine job of laundering Medici's dirty money. But the faces behind the numbers, the names on the dotted lines — they're fakes. Shams. Straw men. Frank Medici signs the checks himself. And now, thanks to Lainey, we can prove it.'

'I hope so,' said Gren. 'Prove it and make it stick. I don't want him coming after my family.'

16

My family. Nikki wrapped both arms around Gren's neck, resting her head against his. From her perch on his lap she could see Lainey, sitting cross-legged in the middle of Noble's bed, smiling and laughing, playing peek-a-boo with Claire for the very first . . . and probably last time.

She could see Sergeant Murphy, slumped in Noble's easy chair, holding an ice bag to his head. The man looked a lot less dangerous with his long legs propped up on the ottoman and his dark hair slightly disheveled. His wistful smile, as he watched Lainey and Claire at play, confirmed he'd begun to feel much more than just a protector's duty toward her sister. That was good. If love really was a mover of mountains, Murphy just might be up to the challenge of Frank Medici.

She could see Noble, too, or the back of him anyway, stooped over the kitchen counter, building a plate of sandwiches that would probably feed a small army. And, as Gren's arms closed around her in a gentle, sheltering embrace, she saw something else — within herself. For the first time in her life, Nikki felt truly safe, wanted, and *loved*.

All her worries about whether or not Gren would understand, whether he'd ever be able to forgive her for keeping secrets and lying, were groundless. All he really needed, he'd said, was to know she and Claire were safe, to know his quest for the truth hadn't caused them any harm. They'd talk it all over if she wanted. Later. But for now it was enough to hold her in his arms. Nikki was inclined to agree.

'How you doin'?' He spoke in an intimate whisper, brushing her cheek with his lips. If she turned, ever so slightly, and tipped her chin just so, those warm, gentle lips of his would find their way to hers. And then . . .

She smiled to herself. There'd be plenty of time for kissing later, without the audience. Plenty of long autumn evenings at home, with nothing to do but kiss, and hold each other, and discover all the wonders of making love.

'I'm doing fine. Better than fine. Oh, Gren, I was so afraid.'

'I know. Me too. But you don't have to be afraid anymore. From what Murphy told me on the way over, his people have all the bases covered. Medici really doesn't know about Claire. Or you, either. And once Lainey testifies, they'll make sure she gets a new life, a new chance.'

'Alone.' Nikki choked back a sob at the thought of Lainey's sacrifice. It was all so unfair.

'I'm not so sure about that.'

'You're not? Why? What do you mean?'

He chuckled, a low, familiar sound that rumbled through her body, sparking something warm and wonderful deep inside. Lowering his voice so only she would hear, he continued. 'I mean, I think she'll have company . . . if Murphy has anything to say about it, that is. Didn't you wonder why he was so insistent about riding over here with me, and sending Lainey with you in the station wagon?'

'Not really. I figured he was just being nice, trying to give us some time alone, y'know, to visit.'

'That was part of it, I suppose. He had a few questions about Noble, wanted to check me out again, too, make absolutely sure they could trust me to keep quiet. I think I convinced him.'

He paused, drawing a deep, halting breath before he continued. 'Nikki, you *do* know you can trust me . . . right?'

She smiled, gently stroking his cheek. 'I know.' It felt so right, so natural. And in the days, months . . . *years* to come, she'd make certain he never had reason to doubt her trust again.

As relief banished the worry lines from his forehead, turning his frown into a lopsided smile, Nikki's heart gave a joyful little leap in her chest. In their short time together she'd somehow learned to love that silly smile.

'Anyway,' continued Gren, 'I think Murphy's real reason for riding with me was to let somebody know his plans, maybe keep you from worrying.' He paused, tenderly kissing her chin, then resting his head on her shoulder.

She nudged him with her elbow. 'Are you going to make me guess?'

He chuckled again. 'Sorry. I was just watching them. Seems Murphy is ready to quit the force. He says if Lainey's willing, that brand new identity of hers is going to include a new husband.'

Nikki gazed across the room at her sister, saw her exchange a bittersweet smile with Murphy, and felt a spark of hope for their future. Maybe there were such things as happy endings.

Murphy pushed to his feet, stepped into the alcove, and bent to whisper something in Lainey's ear. Nikki saw her sister tense, watched her turn and mouth the words *five more minutes*, saw a single tear trickle down her cheek as she pulled Claire into her arms.

The baby squirmed for a moment, then dropped her tiny head onto Lainey's shoulder.

'Almost as if she knows,' said Gren softly.

Nikki swiped at the tears in her own eyes, then pulled free of Gren's embrace, rising stiffly to her feet. She wasn't going to cry. Later, maybe, but not now. She had to be strong, for Lainey.

'We'll be going now,' said Murphy, grim-faced and businesslike once more. Nikki had a feeling it was all an act. After all, a Mountie shouldn't cry on the job.

'Thanks for your hospitality, Mr. Bateman.' Murphy barked the obligatory phrase, then clenched his teeth so tightly the muscles in his jaw began to twitch. Watching, Nikki knew she was right. This was hard for him, too.

'You didn't eat,' exclaimed Noble,

wiping his hands on the front of his overalls as he turned. 'Stay, eat . . . you'll be hungry on the road.'

'I'm sorry, sir, but we really can't spare the time.'

Noble looked as if he might argue the point, but after briefly studying Murphy's stand-at-attention attitude, the old man turned back to the counter and reached for the plastic wrap. 'I'll just pack 'em up for you then. Mark my words, young man, you'll be glad of 'em later on. Maybe a bite of fruit, too . . . '

'We'd appreciate that, sir.'

'I'll say,' said Lainey, crossing the room with Claire in her arms. 'I swear if I have to eat one more fast food burger, I'll pu — ' She caught herself, managing a half-hearted, sheepish grin. 'I'll . . . um . . . uh . . . up-chuck. Whew! Nearly taught the little one a new word.'

Her forced laughter sounded more like a sob to Nikki and she pulled her sister close, hugging the baby between them. Claire giggled and squealed, oblivious to the tears of the two women who held her.

'Enough,' said Lainey at last, relinquishing Claire to Gren's waiting arms. 'I don't want to remember you crying, Cat. And that's not how I want you ... or Claire ... to remember me, either.'

She dried her face on her sleeve, then squared her shoulders. 'Ready, Murph?'

'Any time.'

Nikki let herself lean on Gren as his arm settled comfortably around her shoulders. A deep sigh shuddered through her as she struggled to hold back her tears. This moment was much more than an ending, it was a new beginning. For all of them. Her sister wasn't heading off to face the world alone. She'd have Murphy's strength to lean on, his love to keep her safe.

'This is for you,' said Lainey, slipping a folded piece of pale blue paper into Nikki's hand. 'For both of you — and for Claire.' She smiled up at the baby in Gren's arms, then hastily brushed a tear from her cheek. 'Tell her about her Aunt Lainey, okay? And tell her . . . tell her I loved her.'

Turning, Lainey grabbed Murphy's arm. 'Get me out of here, Murph, before I change my mind.'

'Lainey? Wait!' cried Nikki, afraid for a moment that her sister wouldn't stop to hear what she had to say. Murphy made the decision for her, blocking the doorway, dropping his arm around Lainey's shoulders. She didn't look back.

'Someday,' said Nikki, 'when we're certain it's safe, I'll tell her about her *mother*, and the very brave thing she did for love.'

Wordlessly Lainey pushed through the door, dragging Murphy along with her, walking out of their lives forever.

Noble bustled out after them, passing a bulging, brown paper sack through the car window. 'Can't have you drivin' hungry!' he shouted, waving as Murphy drove away. Shoving his hands deep into the pockets of his overalls, the old man strode off down the laneway and disappeared into his workshop.

'Wise man,' said Gren, kissing Nikki gently on the forehead. 'Remind me to thank him. What's that she gave you?'

Nikki carefully unfolded the single sheet of blue paper.

'A nursery rhyme. We used to say it all the time when we were kids.'

She brushed the tears away, resting her head on Gren's shoulder, smiling when Claire leaned over to grab a fistful of hair — one pain she'd never complain about again.

'I never really thought about what it meant, until now. But Claire will know . . . someday. We'll help her understand.'

'Together?'

Nikki looked up, meeting two pairs of shining eyes, two happy faces . . . her family. 'Together. If you still want us, that is.'

'Forever.' Pulling her close, Gren bent to touch her lips with his and sealed the promise with a kiss.

We do hope that you have enjoyed reading this large print book.

Did you know that all of our titles are available for purchase?

We publish a wide range of high quality large print books including:
Romances, Mysteries, Classics
General Fiction
Non Fiction and Westerns

Special interest titles available in large print are:
The Little Oxford Dictionary
Music Book, Song Book
Hymn Book, Service Book

Also available from us courtesy of Oxford University Press:
Young Readers' Dictionary
(large print edition)
Young Readers' Thesaurus
(large print edition)

For further information or a free brochure, please contact us at:
Ulverscroft Large Print Books Ltd.,
The Green, Bradgate Road, Anstey,
Leicester, LE7 7FU, England.
Tel: (00 44) **0116 236 4325**
Fax: (00 44) **0116 234 0205**